"Cole, We Were A Couple Of Kids Before Who Knew Nothing About What We Wanted In Life,"

Allison said.

"Speak for yourself," Cole replied. "I always knew what I wanted. Nothing's changed."

"I've changed, Cole. I'm not the little pigtailed girl who used to follow you everywhere."

He ran his hand down her side, tracing her curves. "I'll admit to some changes, but I see nothing wrong with them."

"I've been on my own for a long time, Cole. I've learned to appreciate my freedom and independence."

"Do you think I'm asking you to give those up?"

"Aren't you?"

"Hell, no. I'm proud that you found your talents. All I'm saying is that I want you in my life."

Dear Reader,

I know you can't wait to get your hands on September's Silhouette Desire books! First, because September has the latest installment in Diana Palmer's MOST WANTED series—*The Case of the Missing Secretary*. And don't worry if you missed earlier books in the series; each story stands on its own.

Next, because September has Annette Broadrick, and the start of her new series, the SONS OF TEXAS. This month we have *Love Texas Style!* Look for *Courtship Texas Style!* in October and *Marriage Texas Style!* in November.

And, of course, there's this month's thrilling, sexy, wonderful *Man of the Month, Navarrone,* by Helen R. Myers. And September is completed with fabulous stories by Laura Leone, Jean Barrett and a talented newcomer I know you'll love, Mary Maxwell.

Don't miss any of these. I couldn't begin to pick a favorite—they're all so terrific—and I'll bet you couldn't, either.

All the best,

Lucia Macro
Senior Editor

ANNETTE BROADRICK
LOVE TEXAS STYLE!

SILHOUETTE *Desire*®

Published by Silhouette Books New York

America's Publisher of Contemporary Romance

SILHOUETTE BOOKS
300 East 42nd St., New York, N.Y. 10017

LOVE TEXAS STYLE!

ISBN: 0-373-05734-2

First Silhouette Books printing September 1992

All the characters in this book have no existence outside the imagination of the author and have no relation whatsoever to anyone bearing the same name or names. They are not even distantly inspired by any individual known or unknown to the author, and all incidents are pure invention.

Printed in the U.S.A.

ANNETTE BROADRICK

lives on the shores of Lake of the Ozarks in Missouri, where she spends her time doing what she loves most—reading and writing romance fiction. Since 1984, when her first book was published, Annette has been delighting her readers with her imaginative and innovative style. In addition to being nominated by *Romantic Times* magazine as one of the Best New Authors of 1984, she has also won the *Romantic Times* Reviewer's Choice Award for Best in its Series for her novels *Heat of the Night, Mystery Lover* and *Irresistible,* the *Romantic Times* WISH Award for her hero in *Strange Enchantment* and the *Romantic Times* Lifetime Achievement Award for Series Romance.

One

Cole felt the cool rush of water swirl over his feet and eddy around his ankles before the wave ebbed and left him standing on the firmly packed sand once more. Brilliant rays of color shot up into the sky across the wide expanse of the Gulf of Mexico.

Dawn was Cole's favorite time of day, and watching the sun come up from the southern tip of Padre Island off the coast of south Texas was his favorite place to be in the world.

For the first time in a very long while, Cole Callaway felt a sense of peace settle over him. He could feel the tight muscles in his neck and shoulders uncoil and release their tension.

He stood and gazed at the silent, dazzling panoply of brilliant hues splashing the sky with color, changing moment by moment as each ray touched first one cloud lying near the horizon, then another. They appeared to catch fire until the sky turned into a blaze of peach and orange and yellow and gold.

The water continued to soothe his feet and ankles with its soft massage, occasionally splashing as high as the knees of his dress pants. All of his focus remained on the magical splendor displayed around him.

The sun's actual appearance became almost anticlimactic as its fiery brilliance quickly washed the colors until they faded away into muted hues. The waves became more distinct, reflecting the sun's sparkle as they eased into their own colorful display of greens and blues.

Cole released a deep sigh and filled his lungs with the fresh breeze dancing across the water to cool the inhabitants of the island at this early hour. He could feel the new energy swirl into his body... regenerating, cleansing, renewing.

He luxuriated in the moment, knowing that it had been worth the five-hundred-mile drive from Dallas through the night in order to be a witness to this daily ritual of renewal.

Being there, seeing the infinitely varied marvels of nature, helped him view his life from a new perspective, helped him in his search for inner peace.

Somehow no problem appeared insurmountable, no task seemed overwhelming to him whenever he stood beside the sea. Regardless of the number of beaches he'd visited throughout the world, this particular island in this particular part of the world would always represent home to him. His restless spirit found peace on these shores.

Cole had known the night before that he had to get away for a few hours. The pressure had been building within him for weeks with back-to-back meetings and late-night telephone conversations with overseas offices.

No matter how much he attempted to delegate, there always seemed to be decisions that only he could make.

He was so tired. He couldn't remember the last full night's sleep he'd had or the last time he'd been able to enjoy an uninterrupted meal.

Most of his meals were business meetings, in order to fit them all into his schedule. He couldn't remember the last time he'd taken a day off. Hell, he couldn't remember the last time he'd taken a few *hours* off. He felt like a caged animal running inside a spinning wheel. No matter how fast he ran, there seemed to be no end as he circled round and round, faster and faster.

The meeting last night had epitomized the futility of his work as he watched the lack of cohesion among the officers and directors of that particular company. He'd sat there listening to the debates, the accusations, the jockeying for position and power and wondered what he was doing there. With a sense of shock, he suddenly discovered that he had absolutely no interest in the outcome of the heated discussion going on around him.

So he had walked out. He'd gotten into his late-model foreign sports car and headed south on Highway 35E, back to his high-rise condo in Austin. By the time he reached the outskirts—and his turnoff five hours later—he'd already decided to continue south. At first he'd thought about going to the ranch southwest of San Antonio, but when he reached that exit, he ignored it and continued south, on and on into the night, feeling the powerful engine of the car sweep him along.

He had known he was running, escaping, and he didn't care. Somewhere inside of him something had broken loose and had guided him down through the small towns of Kingsville, Raymondville, Harlingen, San Benito, until he slowed, finally for Port Isabel.

Once he reached that small town, whose wide streets were empty at four in the morning, he'd taken the two-mile causeway across to the island and pulled into the parking lot of his condo. The large high rise had been built on the island by one of his companies ten years ago, when the real estate boom had been at its peak.

He'd left his suit coat and tie in the car, taken off his socks and shoes, and headed toward the water. He had no idea how far he'd walked down the beach, but he'd gone far enough to outdistance the line of cars, trucks and campers that were parked along its shore.

He was alone now, except for the water, the sand, the dunes with the smattering of sea grass behind him, and the sun, gilding each thing it touched with its magic as it continued its daily climb into the sky.

The breeze teased at his dark hair, blowing it into his eyes and reminding him that he needed a haircut. He ran his hand through it, tousling it even more. He needed more than a haircut! He needed respite from his life-style.

Most of the time he accepted the role he'd been assigned in life. He never questioned the sometimes gargantuan responsibilities he was expected to deal with on a daily basis. But last night, when he'd gotten up and walked out of the meeting, he'd felt as though he'd walked out on everything—the businesses, the ranch, his two brothers, his maiden aunt—everything he'd carried since he was twenty years old.

He'd been head of the family, head of Callaway Enterprises, for over fifteen years. It seemed like a lifetime... a lifetime alone.

An image appeared for a brief moment in his mind to remind him of all that he had lost. Black eyes stared at him... wide and slightly slanted like a doe's eyes. He could see them in different moods... sparkling with mischief, soft with love and compassion, spitting fire. He could see a pair of lips . . . pouting, smiling with delight, trembling with despair.

Allison.

Just thinking her name provoked a familiar pain in his heart. After all these years he still compared every woman he met with his ideal of what a woman should be.

Once he had almost decided to marry someone else until he realized that he'd been looking for a substitute for Allison, which wasn't fair to either him or the woman he was seeing at the time. Even now, whenever he saw a small black-haired woman with fair skin his heart would leap into his throat for that brief instant when he thought she might possibly be Allison Alvarez.

But she never was.

Allison had disappeared out of his life at a time when he'd needed her the most. How could he forget that? How could he ever forgive her for that? There were times, however, such as now—as he turned to begin the long trek back to the condo—when he admitted to himself that he would have forgiven her anything during these past fifteen years if she had shown up in his life once again.

He reached into his shirt pocket and absently retrieved a cigarette. Placing it in his mouth, he cupped his hand around the end and turned his back to the breeze in order to light it. He filled his lungs with its smoke and immediately began to cough.

Damn! He shook his head with irritation at himself and tossed the offending cylinder into the water. His throat was already raw from too many of them. He had to quit, that was all there was to it. His system was rebelling against several things at the moment, including his lack of rest and his irregular meals.

He stayed at the edge of the water on his return walk, his mind drifting back over the past few days. He wished that his brother, Cameron, had been at the meeting last night. Cameron helped him to keep his perspective. He trusted his brother's judgment and his advice.

Without Cam's strong support, Cole would have walked away years ago... like Cody, their youngest brother, who had refused to have anything to do with the corporation. Cody went his own way without explanation. Perhaps that was why Cole found Cody so irritating at times. If he were to face the truth, he was probably more than a little envious of his baby brother's freedom. He wondered if Cody knew that, or whether he felt that he could never measure up to Cole's expectations.

He shook his head. Cody had only been ten years old when their parents had been killed, much too young to have lost both of them. Cole had tried to make up the loss to both Cam and Cody, but he knew that he'd failed them miserably.

At least Cameron had found contentment in his personal life. At thirty he already had a wife and baby daughter. His degrees in law and accounting made him an invaluable asset to the family holdings.

Cole noticed that a few people were now stirring as he made his way back down the beach. Ahead of him three teenage boys played in the shallows, tossing a Frisbee to each other.

He recalled that this was the week for spring break for many schools. He wished he had the boys' boisterousness, their excessive energy, their sheer enjoyment of being alive. What would it feel like to be without any responsibility except to have fun? Had he ever had such a time in his life?

Once again a face flashed into his memory. Was that why he continued to hold such a special place in his memories for Allison? Was it because she represented the best part of his life, those years when he was growing up, when his parents had been alive, when his life had been truly golden?

He continued walking toward the boys, idly watching their game. The Frisbee flew toward the boy who was directly in front of Cole and he paused, in case the boy started running backward to catch it. The capricious wind caught the airborne missile and lifted it clear of the boy's outstretched hand, carrying it another twenty feet so that Cole only had to reach out a hand to grab it. With an unfamiliar sense of playfulness, he did.

The other two boys began to laugh and dance around in the water, yelling congratulatory remarks, while the third boy, wearing a grin, turned and began to jog toward him. Cole knew he must look ridiculous walking the beach in a dress shirt and slacks soaked to the knees, but somehow it didn't seem to matter. Their enjoyment of the morning was enough to create a bond between him and the boys.

"Say, I'm really sorry," the boy said somewhat out of breath as he came splashing up to Cole. "I missed that one by a mile. I really appreciate..."

His words faded into the sounds of the waves as Cole stared at the young boy in front of him. His hair was the color of wheat, with threads of red and deep gold. Black eyes filled with sparkling glints of humor looked at Cole.

Except for the eye color, he felt as though he were seeing Cody all over again...a teenaged Cody with the same-shaped face, the same expression in his eyes, the same infectious grin, the same hair color...Cody at that gawky adolescent stage where a boy is all knees, elbows and gangly arms and legs.

No. There was no way. Even if Cody had been careless enough to have gotten some girl pregnant, he wasn't old enough to have sired this boy.

Cole became aware he had handed the Frisbee to the boy without saying anything. The boy flashed him another one of those eerily familiar grins and turned away, sailing the Frisbee across the waves to his friends. As though from a distance, Cole heard himself ask, "What's your name, son?"

He heard the authoritarian tone in his voice too late to alter it, and winced. He was so accustomed to demanding answers that he'd almost lost touch with common courtesy. He wanted to apologize, to explain, but didn't know how to begin. He wasn't surprised to see the boy stiffen at his brusque tone of voice.

The boy stopped and slowly turned around. "Tony," the boy replied shortly.

Before Tony had time to leave, Cole stuck out his hand and smiled in an effort to counteract his earlier curtness. "I'm glad to meet you, Tony. I'm Cole Callaway."

Tony had already backed up several steps when he heard Cole's name. He stopped dead and stared at the man before him. Slowly he took the necessary steps to reach Cole's hand. He shook it slowly and said, "You mean you're *the* Cole Callaway?"

Cole could hear equal parts of awe and curiosity in the boy's voice and felt an unreasoning sense of elation because he recognized his name. "As far as I know, I'm the only one around."

"The one who's planning to run for governor? The guy with all the—" He stopped, as though embarrassed at what he'd almost said.

Tony had a firm grip, a man's grip. Cole glanced down at the hand that seemed too large and strong for the boy's body. With a vague sense of reluctance he let go of the boy's hand and said, "There's nothing official about my political plans as yet, Tony. But that never stops the media from speculating."

"Wow! It's great to meet you, Mr. Callaway."

"Same here, Tony." As casually as possible he asked, "Your last name is?"

"Alvarez, sir. Tony Alvarez."

The words hit Cole like a massive blow to the midsection. For a brief moment Cole felt as though he were reeling. He felt like doubling over in an effort to protect his midriff from another assault.

Tony Alvarez. A name from the past . . . belonging to a boy who wore the stamp of the Callaways all over him.

He closed his eyes for a moment in an effort to get his bearings while his mind screamed out denials— No! *No! It couldn't be! It wasn't possible, it couldn't be possible!*—while all the time Cole knew with an inner certainty that of course it was true.

"Is something wrong, Mr. Callaway?" Tony sounded puzzled.

Cole shook his head, trying to clear it of the buzzing sound that seemed to ring in his ears.

"Um, no, son. Nothing's wrong. I guess you caught me by surprise. I once knew a Tony Alvarez, a long time ago."

The boy's grin grew wider. "No kidding? Wouldn't that be something if it was my grandfather? Mom named me after him. He died before I was born, and she said she wanted to keep his name alive."

One last question. "How old are you? I would guess you're around sixteen or so."

Tony laughed. "Yeah, that's what everybody thinks. I guess I'm just big for my age. I'm fourteen; I'll be fifteen in July. I've always looked older."

So it was true. The implications of all that Cole was hearing seemed to beat at him from every direction. "You live around here, Tony?" Cole managed to ask, his voice sounding hoarse in his ears. He began to walk toward the other boys who were obviously puzzled by Tony's prolonged conversation with a stranger.

"Uh, no, sir. We just came down here for a few days. My mom and I live in a little town called Mason in central Texas. She owns an art gallery there." With obvious pride he continued, "She's an artist and sculptor. She's won lots of awards. Several of her sculptures are on display at the Cowboy Artists of America Museum in Kerrville."

A sudden vision of a sculpture he'd recently purchased for his office flashed into Cole's mind. Wild horses raced down a rocky incline, their manes and hooves flying. He'd been mesmerized by the freedom, the life, and the artistic splendor of the piece. The sculpture had been signed "A. Alvarez."

"Allison." He heard his voice as if it were independent of him, speaking her name out loud for the first time in years. She'd been here in Texas all along, no more than a hundred miles from his place in Austin.

"That's right. That's my mom's name. Do you know her?"

"I recently bought one of her sculptures," he responded, sidestepping the question.

"No kidding? Wow, that's neat! I'll have to tell her." Tony saw his buddies standing there waiting for him. He glanced back at Cole and added, "And I'll have to tell her about meeting you."

Cole could think of a dozen rejoinders to that remark, none of them suitable for this boy to hear.

My God! How could he possibly deal with this shock without giving himself away? He had to be alone for a while, a few hours at least, to try to come to grips with the information he'd just been given. "Are you going to be around awhile?" he asked casually.

"Yeah. We just got here yesterday. We'll be here until the end of the week."

"Then I'll probably see you again," he offered quietly, thankful that he'd been granted a reprieve.

Cole found his way back to the high rise by force of habit. He needed a drink. As soon as he let himself into the hallway of the large penthouse suite, he headed for the bar.

Cole had never been one to drink much because he preferred to keep a clear head. However, he knew he needed help in dealing with the shock he'd just received.

The phone rang.

He knew the caller had to be family. The phone number to the condo was a closely guarded secret. Only an emergency would have prompted someone to call him, particularly since he hadn't told anyone where he would be. How could he? He hadn't known himself.

He picked up the phone and growled, "Yes?"

"Cole! Thank God I found you! I've been looking everywhere. The last anyone knew you walked out in the middle of a meeting in Dallas and somehow managed to disappear. I'd about given up when I remembered the beach place."

"Okay, Cody, you found me. What's wrong?"

"Cole, I'm afraid I've got some really bad news. Man, I hate to break it to you like this, but—"

"Something's happened to Aunt Letty?" She was only in her mid-fifties, and Cole would have thought she was too ornery to die this young, but as shaken as Cody sounded, Cole knew the news was bad.

"Aunt Letty's fine, Cole. I'm afraid it's Cameron and Andrea."

Stark terror swept over him. "What! What are you talking about? What happened?"

"They were on their way out to the ranch last night to pick up Trisha from Aunt Letty's. There was a car accident, Cole. Nobody seems to know exactly what happened. Maybe a deer was in the road. The car was discovered around midnight last night."

"How bad is it, Cody? Tell me!"

"Uh, Andrea's dead, Cole. Cameron's been in surgery since they brought him in. He's in critical condition."

"Where are you now?"

"At Methodist Hospital in San Antonio."

"Call Pete and have him pick me up in the helicopter."

"Right away, Cole."

They hung up. Cole slowly sank to the edge of the couch and stared across the room at the fully stocked bar. He'd been going to have a drink because...because he didn't know how to handle the shock he'd just had. And now...he discovered his brother was in critical condition in San Antonio, his sister-in-law dead. A drink wasn't going to help him deal with any of this.

He strode into the master bedroom and stripped out of his clothes. He couldn't remember the last time he'd been to bed. None of that mattered now. He had to get to Cameron. He needed to be there for his brother, regardless of what else was happening in his life.

And the baby. He'd forgotten to ask Cody if Letty was at the hospital or whether she was still at the ranch with Trisha.

Dear God. Trisha was less than a year old. She'd just lost her mother and possibly her father in the same kind of accident that had taken her grandparents' lives fifteen years before.

What was happening? Were the Callaways cursed? Was history repeating itself?

Cole stepped off the elevator onto the surgical floor and started toward the nurses' station. After less than a half-dozen steps he spotted Cody pacing in a small waiting room. He veered to join him.

"Any word?"

"None."

"Damn."

"I know."

"When did you get here?"

"As soon as I got the call last night. The Highway Patrol had been alerted by a passing motorist who saw the car and stopped to render assistance. According to the police report, Andrea was killed on impact."

Cole rubbed the bridge of his nose with his thumb and forefinger. "Damn, that's tough. How about Cam?"

"He'd been knocked unconscious, which was probably a blessing. He has a broken arm and leg, concussion, busted ribs and possible internal injuries. With surgery taking this long, I would say that was a safe bet."

"Has he regained consciousness enough to explain what happened?"

"No. According to the report, from the skid marks it looked as though Cameron had tried to stop, tried to swerve or attempted to maneuver past something in the road and lost control of the car. The deer are so plentiful in that area, it could easily have been one of them.''

''Was there any sign of a deer having been hit?''

''Not that the Highway Patrol spotted.''

Cole began to pace while Cody watched him. ''We've got to do something,'' Cole muttered after a long silence.

''I know what you're feeling, Cole. I've already worn a path in the tile since I got here. I tried to think of where you would be, then I'd stop and call. I guess I must have left messages all over the state of Texas.''

Cole stopped pacing and glanced at his younger brother. He looked like hell. ''When's the last time you got some sleep?''

Cody shrugged.

''Why don't you stretch out over there on that couch? I'll wake you when there's any word.''

Cody shook his head. ''I can't. Every time I shut my eyes I see the remains of Cameron's car. The wrecker was just getting there when I drove past the accident site on my way into town. That damned little foreign car looked like a giant had stomped on it!'' He shook his head in despair. ''I always told Cam he needed to get something safer on the road, but he never listened to me. What did I know, a snot-nosed kid who'd pestered him all his life—''

''He's going to be all right,'' Cole said in a soothing voice. He went over and sat beside Cody. ''He's tough, our brother. Don't you know that by now? Nobody's going to stop us. We're the Three Musketeers, remember?''

Cody slowly nodded. ''Yeah. You used to tell me that story when I was a kid.''

"All for one and one for all. That's the Callaway motto. Cameron's going to make it. We're going to be right there, on either side of him, making sure he does."

Cole met Cody's anguished expression with a calmness he was far from feeling. He deliberately sat back in his chair. There was nothing he could do for Cameron. The best doctors around were working on him at the moment.

Now he had to look after Cody. He had to distract him in some way. Although he hadn't had much time to think about what he'd just learned about his own past—in fact, he was still reeling from the shock—he knew he could discuss anything with Cody because he was family.

"I got hit with some news this morning, just before you called," Cole began slowly, feeling his way into the labyrinth of painful and confused emotions. "It has certainly given me a brand-new perspective on my life."

Cody had been studying his hands and popping his knuckles when Cole spoke. He gave Cole a look that revealed his sudden awareness of Cole's peculiar tone. "Yeah? What's that?"

"I just found out that I have a fourteen-year-old son who I never knew existed."

Two

"Allison? Can you keep a secret?" Cole felt so grown-up now that he had started the first grade and was away from the ranch each day. The thing was, he missed his four-year-old companion, who had gamely followed him around the ranch as far back as he could remember. She had met him as soon as he'd gotten home that afternoon. He could hardly wait to show her what he'd found that morning before going off to school.

She was dressed identically to him in shirt, jeans and scuffed boots. She wore her hair in braids that bounced on her shoulders as she skipped to keep up with his longer stride. Her black eyes registered her curiosity as she stared up at him from beneath a thick fringe of hair.

"'Course I can keep a secret," she replied with the proper amount of disgust that he might think otherwise. "What is it?"

He continued to the barn where he'd followed the cat early this morning. "You'll see," he said with a grin, enjoying the mystery. Once inside the barn he led the way toward the storage side of the big building. He paused at the bottom of the ladder that led up into the hayloft and pressed his finger to his lips.

She silently nodded her head in understanding. Cole gingerly climbed the rungs until he could peer into the loft. As soon as he saw that the coast was clear, he crawled onto the wooden flooring and turned, waiting.

Allison didn't disappoint him. She was determinedly climbing the steep rungs, her bottom lip caught between her teeth in concentration, her eyes huge in her white face. By the time she reached his side she was trembling, but she hadn't made a single protest at the height or the scary climb.

Still on his hands and knees, he crawled to the corner of the loft. Allison followed. When he stopped and pointed, she leaned over his shoulder fearfully. Her look of surprise and pleasure had been worth his sharing his secret with her. He sat back with a grin on his face.

"How many is there?" she whispered.

He held up three fingers.

"Where's the momma?"

"I dunno, but she wouldn't like it if she knew we found her hidin' place. She'd prob'ly move 'em."

They inched away as silently as they had come. When they reached the ladder Cole went first to make sure the coast was clear. Both of them had strict instructions *not* to attempt to climb up into the loft. Once down, he waited impatiently for Allison to feel her way, rung by rung, to the bottom.

As soon as her feet touched the ground she spun around, her expressive eyes mirroring her delight. ''We've got kittens!''

He nodded, feeling very important to have found them on his own.

''Can we keep them?''

''I dunno. Maybe so.''

''Have you touched them?''

He shook his head. ''The momma would smell me on her babies and wouldn't like it. I think they just got bornded.''

''Oh, Cole, I want one for my very own.''

''Maybe your mom and dad will let you have one for your birthday.''

She clapped her hands. ''Do you really think so?''

''I'll ask.''

Later he had asked his dad if he could give one of the barn kittens to Allison for her fifth birthday. After reprimanding him for climbing up into the loft, his dad had insisted he check with Tony and Kathleen, her parents. Tony was the boss around the ranch. His dad called him the foreman. Cole had always been in awe of Tony. He was dark and never said much, but Cole knew that he was just about the greatest cowboy who ever lived, and he ran the Circle C ranch. Kathleen was easier to talk to. She and his mother could have been sisters, with their fair skin and reddish-blond hair. She was always laughing and talking and hugging people. She had laughingly agreed that what Allison needed more than anything for her birthday was a kitten.

She had picked the tiger-striped one who would grow into a big old tomcat.

Allison named him Crybaby.

* * *

By the time he was ten, Cole had more important things to do than to hang around with a girl, even Allison. He'd been sneaking away from the house one hot afternoon when he discovered that Allison was following him.

Disgusted, he turned and confronted her. "How come you have to follow me everywhere I go?"

"'Cause I want to," Allison replied nonchalantly. "'Sides, I figger you're goin' out to where my daddy is." She stuck her hands in her jeans pockets. "I was just goin' to go find him."

"Well, you're not goin' to find him following me around," he pointed out with ill-concealed irritation. "He and Dad left in the pickup to go check on part of the ranch."

Allison stared at him without saying anything more, the expression in her black eyes silently eloquent.

He couldn't stand it when she looked at him like that. She always made him feel so mean. The problem was that there was nobody else on the ranch besides him for her to play with. Cameron was barely five. He knew she got bored, just as he did. Her mother spent a lot of her time resting. His mom was busy taking care of Cameron and getting ready for the new baby's arrival as well as running the Big House. His Aunt Letty was never any fun, always scolding him for making too much noise or for asking so many questions. He'd left the house to stay out of trouble and he'd made up his mind about what he planned to do with the rest of his day. Now here was Allison wanting to tag along.

"Oh, all right," he said disgustedly. "Come on. But you gotta promise not to tell anybody where we're going, because it's my secret place and nobody knows about it."

"Couldn't we go ridin'?"

"No. Remember my dad said we can't ride unless your dad's here to supervise."

She grinned. "That's 'cause my dad's the best rider in the whole wide world. He's got lots of trophies and medals and things to prove it."

Cole was much more comfortable with Antonio Alvarez now that he was older, but he still admired him tremendously. He'd seen all the rodeo medals Tony had won before Cole's dad had coaxed him into taking over the running of the ranch. That was several years before Cole was born.

His mom had told him how his dad and Tony had become close friends when they'd been in the army in Korea. Now she and Tony's wife were good friends, too.

He just wished that Allison had been a boy so he would have had someone fun to play with. Of course she really wasn't all that bad—for a girl. She could run and could draw her toy pistol almost as fast as he could. She wasn't afraid of nothing. The only time he'd seen her cry was once when he told her he didn't want to play with her because she was a girl and that she had to go home and leave him alone.

Boy, her tears had really upset him. He hadn't meant what he'd said anyway. He'd just been in a bad mood because Aunt Letty had sent him out of the house.

After that one time when he'd made Allison cry, Cole had been more careful about taking his bad feelings out on her.

"So, are you comin' or not?"

"Where you goin'?"

"Swimming."

Her eyes lighted up. "Really? Where?" She glanced around the ranch buildings.

"It's a secret place. Only me and my dad know about it. He takes me there whenever he can spare the time. You still want to go?" he asked.

She nodded emphatically.

"It's a long walk. Usually my dad takes me by horseback." He pointed in the direction he'd been going when he heard her behind him. "See those trees back up in the hills over there?" he pointed.

"Uh-huh."

"There's a creek along there. My dad says that it must have gotten dammed up one winter when it flooded and some dead trees got washed downstream. They got caught at a bend in the creek bed and just stayed there. Now, there's this neat place to swim." He looked at her with a slight frown on his face. "You do know how to swim, don't you?"

She nodded her head vigorously but wouldn't meet his eyes.

He sighed. "C'mon, Allison, tell me the truth."

She hung her head, staring at her toes. Uh-oh. She didn't get that hunch-shouldered look very often, but when she did, he knew she was upset. What if she started to cloud up on him and cry again?

"I could teach ya, if ya want," he offered in a gentle voice.

Her head jerked up and she stared at him, the beginning of joy dawning on her face. "Will ya? Really?"

"Sure. My dad showed me. It's not all that hard."

She wrapped her arms around her waist and gave a quick twirl. "That'd be fun!"

The more he thought about it, the better he liked the idea. They could make a day of it and stay out of everybody's way. "I tell you what," he said, already planning their adventure. "I'm going to go into the kitchen without Aunt Letty catching me and ask Conchita to pack us a picnic. A man gets real hungry after swimming." He mimicked his dad's tone of voice as well as his words. "Girls prob'ly get hungry, too. You stay here. I'll be back as soon as I can."

By the time they reached the creek, both of them were hot, tired and hungry. "My dad says you can't go in swimming right after you eat. You might get a cramp," Cole explained as soon as they sat in the shade of a large oak tree.

"What's a cramp?"

"Well, it could be one of those things that live in the water that pinch you."

"Like a crab?"

He nodded. "Something like that."

She peered into the water. "But how does it know if you ate or not?"

"Who knows? But that's what dad says."

"Oh." She looked terribly disappointed.

"But we could maybe drink something," he offered.

"That sounds good."

He unpacked two small cans of fruit juice that Conchita had placed in his knapsack, along with sandwiches, potato chips and cookies. "Here. We'll drink these and rest for a minute, okay?"

When they'd finished their drinks, Allison looked at him. "Now what do we do?"

"Well, first we take off our clothes."

She glanced down at her shirt, jeans and boots. "All of them?" she asked dubiously.

"Well, of course all of them. You wouldn't take a bath in your clothes, would you?" She shook her head. "Well,

swimming's the same thing...except it's lots more fun."
He immediately sat and pulled off his boots.

She did the same.

He unsnapped his jeans, slid them off his hips, then off his legs.

Slowly Allison did the same.

He stood and took off his shirt.

So did she.

They stood there in their underwear and socks and looked at each other.

He shrugged and turned away. Sliding his briefs off, then tugging his socks off as well, he tossed them onto his pile of clothes and determinedly marched bare-bottomed toward the water.

Allison giggled.

He glanced around. "What's wrong with you?"

She covered her mouth but another giggle escaped. "You look so funny."

"No funnier 'n you."

"You're all brown except your bottom."

Girls were so silly. "That's because I'm out in the sun a lot. Are you comin', or not?"

Hastily Allison slid out of her undies and socks and gingerly walked over to join him. He took her hand and carefully led her into the stream.

"It's cold!" she exclaimed as soon as her feet touched the water.

"It's supposed to be," he said with irritation. "That's why it feels so good on a hot day, my dad always says." He continued to lead her into the water until it was up to her waist. "Okay, Allison. Now, I want you to lean back in the water like it's a bed."

"But Cole, I'll drown!"

"No, you won't, you silly! I'm going to have my arms under you." He held his arms straight out in the water where he knelt beside her. "I won't let you drown."

"Promise."

He looked her straight in the eye. "I promise."

Gingerly she lowered herself in the water, her eyes growing bigger and bigger. He continued to hold her. It was easy in the water. Finally she allowed her legs to drift up until she was floating.

"See how easy that is?"

She smiled. "It's easy because you're holding me."

"Not anymore. My arms are underneath you in case you go down, but they're not touching you."

"You won't let me go under?"

"No way." He waited until she began to relax before he said, "Now you gotta turn over and put your face in the water."

"No!" She came to her feet, spluttering and splashing.

He put his hands on his hips. "All right, Allison Alvarez. Do you want me to teach you to swim or not?"

She nodded.

"Then you're going to have to trust me."

"I do trust you," she insisted.

"Then do what I say. I won't ever hurt you. You know that."

She smiled at him, a smile so sweet that he remembered it for years. "I know, Cole."

"Whoopee!" cried Cole a few weeks later. "Allison! My dad just called from the hospital. I have another brother. They're going to call him Cody."

He'd come racing out of the house, yelling his news.

Her smile was wistful. "You got what you wanted. Another brother."

"Well, I don't guess a sister would have been all that bad," he admitted.

"What did Cameron have to say when you told him?"

Cole grinned. "He was disappointed. He was hoping she would have a puppy!"

They both laughed.

"You're really lucky, Cole. I'd give anything to have a sister or a brother. I wouldn't even care which one."

Cole touched her shoulder gently. "Maybe one of these days you'll get your wish."

She shook her head. "I don't think so. I asked Mom once. She said she'd had some problems when I was born. They told her she wouldn't have any more kids."

"Gee, I'm sorry, Allison."

"Me, too."

She looked so downcast that he immediately searched for a way to cheer her up. He knew just the thing. "Would you like to go swimming?"

She glanced up toward the hills. "You mean now?"

"Why not? Dad won't be home until later, and Aunt Letty doesn't care where I am so long as I'm not underfoot."

She nodded. "All right. I'll go get my suit on and meet you out back." She had insisted on having a bathing suit before going swimming again, which he thought was funny, since he'd already seen her without one. She made him wear one, as well. Who could figure girls out, anyway?

Cole was pleased with his student. They had spent the summer going to the creek as often as they could. Allison was no longer afraid of the water, although she still didn't like sticking her face in it.

Later, while they sat on the side of the bank tossing small pebbles into the water, Allison said, "You know, Cole, I'm really lucky to have you in my life. You're like the brother I never had."

"And you're like the sister I never had."

"I'll always think of you as my brother."

"Whenever you need me, I'll be there for you. Don't ever forget that."

Cole had been fourteen the night his father said to him, immediately after dinner, "Son, I need to speak with you. Let's go into my office."

Cole looked at his mother, then at the rest of the family seated around the table. No one seemed to think his dad's request was unusual.

"What's wrong, Dad?" he asked, looking at his father. His dad shook his head and got up from the table.

His mother began to clear the table without saying anything. With a shrug, Cole followed his father out of the room. When they entered the office, his dad nodded toward the fireplace chairs.

"You know, son," he began when they were both seated, "sometimes it's hard to explain why some things happen in life."

Alarmed, Cole said, "What's the matter, Dad? What's happened?"

"Tony and Kathleen got some bad news today from the doctor. It seems that Kathleen has inoperable cancer. They only give her a few weeks to live."

Cole stared at his dad in horror. "You mean Allison's mother is dying?"

"Yes, son. I'm afraid so. I know that you and Allison are close. They intend to tell her tonight and suggested that I explain to you, so that you will understand what she's going through.''

Cole could feel a knot forming in his throat. He was having trouble swallowing. ''Isn't there anything the doctors can do?''

''They said it's too far gone . . . pretty much throughout her system. She hasn't been feeling well for some time. Perhaps if she'd gone in for an earlier checkup, something might have been done. But no one can possibly know for sure.''

Cole hurt. He really liked Mrs. Alvarez. She'd always been friendly to him. She never yelled at him. Tears began to well up in his eyes.

''These things are tough to take, but you needed to know. Allison is going to need a friend.''

''I'll always be her friend, Dad. *Always.*''

''What in the world do you see in Rodney Snyder?'' Cole demanded as Allison's date drove away. He'd been sitting beneath one of the trees near the driveway, waiting for her to come home. He'd gotten up as soon as she started down the lane toward the house she and her father still shared.

He didn't know what her dad was thinking of, letting her date a senior in high school when she was only a sophomore. Why, Rodney was *his* age, much too old for her.

Allison had jumped when he first spoke, and he realized that she hadn't seen him until then.

''Why shouldn't I? At least he notices me and invites me out.''

''What's that supposed to mean? I notice you, don't I?''

She turned away and continued down the lane.

"Well, don't I?" he demanded, following her.

She glanced over her shoulder. "How could you possibly have time for me with all the other girls you're seeing? If your mother had any idea you were out with some of those girls, she'd have a fit."

"We're not talking about me. I want to talk about you."

She continued walking. "Well, I don't want to talk to you!"

"That's been obvious for the past six months, and I don't understand why. What have I done that makes you treat me like poison? I thought we were friends!"

He'd stopped walking so that she had taken several steps ahead of him. The bright moonlight gave enough light so that they were able to see each other. Allison turned and looked at Cole standing there, his hands resting at his sides, his legs slightly apart.

Slowly she walked back to him. "You don't have a clue, do you?" she finally said.

He shook his head.

"I've known you all my life and I feel that I know everything about you, but you don't know me at all," she finally said.

"That's not true. I know more about you than anyone else does." He paused, then drawled, "Unless, of course, you're in the habit of going skinny-dipping with every guy you meet."

"Oh, for Pete's sake, Cole. I was eight years old at the time. Aren't you ever going to let me live that down?"

He grinned. "I doubt it. It's a surefire way to get you riled, and it's powerfully hard to resist the temptation."

Allison clasped her elbows and began walking over to the corral beside the barn. She leaned against the wooden fence. "You don't know anything about my feelings, about my thoughts. All you know about is the tomboy who used to follow you around this place—" she waved her hand to encompass the multitude of buildings that constituted the ranch headquarters "—like I was some kind of pet dog."

"Is that what this is all about? You feel that I've been taking you for granted?"

"Yes! No! Oh, I don't know. It's everything. I'm just tired of all the girls at school trying to be my friend in hopes I'll invite them out here. You're such a big man on campus—class president, football captain, honor student. Not only are you Cole Callaway of *the* Callaways, but you have to make sure you're the best at everything you do!"

"Is that so wrong?"

"Of course not! That's what a Callaway's supposed to do."

"Then I don't see the problem."

"You wouldn't, of course."

"So explain it in simple enough terms so that I can understand."

She turned away and looked out into the pasture. "What were you doing waiting up for me tonight?"

"I was worried about you."

Without looking at him, she said, "Why?"

"Because Snyder's got a well-deserved reputation where girls are concerned. I didn't want him taking advantage of you."

She turned so that she was facing him. "That's a laugh, coming from you."

"What does that mean?"

"You think Rodney's got a reputation? Why, *you're* the one everybody's talking about. I get to hear all the whisperings among the older girls, and the younger ones all want to know what it's like to kiss you."

"What! What kind of question is that?"

"Along the same line as the one Rodney asked tonight when I finally had to tell him to keep his hands to himself. 'If you put out for Callaway, why not me?'" She angled her chin so that the moonlight fell full on her face and for the first time Cole saw the silver streaks down her cheeks where the tears had made their paths.

"Oh, Allison, don't cry," he said, pulling her into his arms and holding her against his shoulder. She felt so good pressed to him like that. "I'll find that son of a—I'll find him tomorrow and beat him to a pulp. How dare he treat you like that? He had no right!"

Her voice sounded muffled in his shirt when she said, "Everybody thinks we're sleeping together, didn't you know? They figure I'm part of the hired help out here. My dad's the foreman, you're the owner's son. What could be more convenient?"

"Who's saying that about you? I want to know who. I'll talk to each one of them. I'll tell them—"

"Nobody's going to believe you, Cole. Don't you understand? Nobody's going to believe a word you say because they know—they *know*—how I feel about you. Everybody knows...but you."

Cole stiffened, then stared down at the top of her head. Her face was still burrowed into his chest. Her voice was muffled. Surely she hadn't said what he thought he heard. Surely she—

"Allison?"

She didn't answer him.

"Look at me. Please."

Slowly she raised her head and looked at him. The tears still slipped silently down her cheeks.

The sudden rush of feeling that hit him almost brought him to his knees. This was Allison—the little girl in pigtails, jeans and boots who had dogged his footsteps for years. Allison—his friend. Allison—his love.

"Oh, baby, I didn't know," he whispered, his voice choked with emotion.

She looked away. "It doesn't matter."

He chuckled. "Doesn't it?"

"Of course not."

"Listen, Miss Haughty Allison Alvarez, it makes a very big difference to me how you feel. So why haven't you told me before?"

"Because you were too busy with all those other girls."

"Do I detect jealousy in that statement?"

"No!"

"So what if I told you that none of those other girls ever made a difference to me? What if I told you that there's only been one girl who matters to me, only one girl I've ever wanted to have as a permanent part of my life?"

She looked back up at him, her gaze intense. "Don't tease me, Cole. Please. If our friendship ever meant anything to you, don't use it against me now."

He leaned down and placed his lips delicately against hers, the first kiss they had ever shared. For a brief moment he felt her grow still. Then she stiffened and pulled away from him.

"What's the matter? Don't you like me to kiss you?"

"You don't have to humor me like a child, Cole. I'm well aware that you think of me like a sister."

He grinned. "Oh, so *that's* it. You don't appreciate my brotherly kiss. In that case, how about this one?"

Cole put every ounce of seductive expertise he'd gained during the past two years into that kiss. At first he wanted to hold back because he didn't want to frighten her, but as soon as he opened his mouth over hers she melted against him. By the time the kiss ended, they were both shaking.

"You'd better go inside now. Tony will be worrying about you."

"But, Cole—"

"I mean it. Get inside. We've got to be careful or things will get out of hand before we're ready. I've still got four years of school back East. You've got to finish high school and plan for college, and then—"

"Cole. What are you talking about?"

"I'm talking about the fact that you're now my girl, from this moment on. I just put my brand on you. I don't want another man to touch you, but I'm not going to take advantage of your lack of experience, either. You hear me? You're too young. Besides, we've got plenty of time. We've got the rest of our lives."

"You mean we're going steady now?"

"That's exactly what I mean."

"So you aren't going to see Darlene or Peggy Sue or Jennifer again?"

He grinned. "I didn't know you knew I was seeing them."

"I know everything you do."

"Everything?"

"That's right."

"Somehow I doubt it, but we'll let it go for now. So do you want to go with me to the senior prom?"

"I'd be honored, Cole."

"Good. Now go inside." He planted a quick kiss on her lips, spun around and loped back to the Big House. She was a temptation few men could resist. But like his dad said, she deserved his love and his respect. He could wait until they were married to make love to her. He'd waited for her this long. What was a few more years?

It was the blackest day of his life.

Cole left the Big House through one of the rear entrances. He didn't want to see anybody. He sure as hell didn't want to talk to anybody. He'd changed out of his suit as soon as the remaining members of the immediate family had returned from the cemetery.

Now he wore his faded jeans, one of his old chambray shirts and his scuffed boots. He made his way to the barn to the four-year-old gelding his dad had given to him two years ago for graduation. With an ease of long practice he placed the blanket, saddle and bridle on him, stepped into the stirrup and left the main headquarters of the ranch.

He couldn't face any more people saying the same things over and over. He couldn't watch the pain and bewilderment in Cameron's and little Cody's faces. He couldn't bear to listen to his Aunt Letty's voice telling yet another person how she had warned her brother over and over that he drove too fast and how he never listened to her.

He had to get away from them all.

He rode for hours. Had anyone asked him later where he'd been, he couldn't have explained. He had taken one last ride with his father.

"Dad, how could you do this to me?" he said at one point. "I need you so much. You've always been here for me, no matter what problems I had. Remember when we used to ride out like this, just the two of us? You answered all my questions, no matter how trivial. You made me proud of my heritage, proud of my land, proud to be a part of the Callaway dynasty."

He hadn't cried when his Aunt Letty had called him at
college in the East, where he was in his second year of
school, and told him what had happened. He hadn't cried
when he arrived home and saw the devastation of his
family and the Circle C employees. His aunt told him that
as head of the family he was expected to help with the
arrangements, which he did. He greeted hundreds of
people who had come to pay their last respects to one of
the legendary figures of Texas. He stood beside the dou-
ble graves and stoically watched his mother and father
being put to rest.

Despite the crowd of people, despite the fact that he
had a brother standing close on either side of him and his
aunt immediately behind him, Cole felt alone.

He wasn't ready for this. His dad was supposed to have
lived for years and years. He'd been in his prime. He
didn't deserve to die. Not now. Cole didn't want to be the
head of the family. He still had two more years of school
and then on to graduate school. He and his dad had
carefully mapped out his education and career. He was
his father's son. He would follow in his father's footsteps. But not now, dear God! Not yet.

Eventually the horse paused and drank from a stream
in the hills. Cole looked around and realized that he was
at his old swimming place, his secret place—the place
where his dad had first brought him as a young boy,
teaching him to swim, teaching him, through example,
how to be a man.

Whether or not Cole liked it, the lessons were con-
cluded. From now on, he was on his own.

On impulse, Cole climbed down. Although it was October, the day was hot. He sat on the bank of the stream
and pulled off his boots and socks. He intended to cool
off by dipping his feet in the water. Once he was bare-

foot, he decided to go into the water. He jerked off his shirt and shucked his jeans and briefs. In minutes he was completely submerged in the water.

Over the years he and his dad had enlarged the pond, making it deeper, turning it into a reservoir where the cattle sometimes came. Now Cole allowed himself to remember the many happy times he'd spent here with his dad . . . and with Allison.

He'd seen Allison at the funeral, sitting beside her father. They hadn't talked much this time. When Cole had left for school in August he'd had a tough time leaving her, which irritated him. He didn't want anyone to have that sort of control of him. Not even Allison.

So he had avoided her on this trip, feeling too vulnerable, his emotions too raw to be controlled.

He swam until his muscles quivered with exhaustion, until he could think of nothing but his aching body. When he knew that he could not lift his arms for another stroke he allowed his feet to sink to the bottom of the pond and began to walk to the bank.

That was when he saw Allison sitting quietly beside his pile of clothes, watching him.

"I thought I might find you here," she said as he paused at the sight of her.

"What are you doing here?"

"I was worried about you."

"Don't be. I can take care of myself." He stood where he was, in waist-deep water.

"I never said you couldn't, Cole." She made no effort to leave.

He pushed his hair out of his face with both hands, slicking it back over his head. "Look, Allison, I'm not dressed for conversation at the moment. Why don't I meet you back at the house later?"

"You can't show me anything I haven't already seen," she pointed out with a half smile.

He wasn't in the mood for games. "Fine." He stalked out of the water, directly toward her.

He knew exactly what he looked like. His body had begun to fill out during the past two years. Since he hadn't been working around the ranch, he'd started working out in the gym at school, keeping his body toned. He didn't need her suddenly widened eyes to remind him that there was a considerable difference between a child of ten and a man of twenty.

She hastily averted her gaze, staring up at the trees that surrounded them. He took his time drying off with his shirt, pulling on his briefs and jeans, then sprawling beside her on the grassy slope. He folded his arms behind his head and lay back, closing his eyes.

He must have fallen asleep because the next time he opened his eyes, shadows had begun to form around them and a breeze whispered among the leaves of the trees.

Allison had stretched out beside him and was fast asleep.

He could count on the fingers of one hand the number of times he'd seen her asleep. Most of the times had been when she and Cole had gone camping with their fathers. The men enjoyed getting away and the children loved to tag along.

They hadn't camped in several years. Now the eighteen-year-old beauty beside him bore little resemblance to the dirty-faced little girl with the long black pigtails who had gone camping with him.

He stared at her, enjoying the chance to study her. Her skin was creamy, like the soft-textured petal of a magnolia. Her black brows made a startling contrast, tilted at each end, giving her the look of a startled doe. Long black lashes brushed against her flushed cheeks. He had an almost irresistible desire to trace the bridge of her nose, following it to the slight tilt at the end.

Her lips were the color of raspberries and looked ripe and succulent. He knew their taste by heart. In the two years since he'd first kissed her, they had spent hours exploring each other, kissing and touching, but he never took advantage of his knowledge and experience. He knew when to stop, knew when he had to clamp down on his own emotions so as not to complete what they had started.

He recognized that he was suddenly famished for the taste of her lips and, yielding to temptation, he leaned over her supine body and kissed her tenderly on the mouth.

She stirred, arching her back slightly so that her full luscious breasts shifted, drawing his attention. She was a gorgeous woman, from the top of her glossy black hair all the way down to her tiny waist, curving hips and thighs, slender ankles and finely arched feet.

He wanted her so much.

When he kissed her a second time, he was having trouble with his breathing.

She shifted so that she was facing him and, still without opening her eyes, drew him into her arms. He pulled her to him, holding her fiercely against him. She sighed and he deepened the kiss. Eventually he had to ease his grip so that they could both breathe.

She opened her eyes and gazed at him from those black depths that seemed to harbor her soul. "Oh, Cole, I've missed you," she whispered, running her hand down his chest. His skin retracted everywhere she touched.

"You're cold," she said.

"I'm burning up," he replied.

She smiled. "Show me."

They both knew that today was different. They had left childhood behind. He pulled the snaps apart on her shirt, then reached inside and unfastened her bra. He nuzzled her breasts, feeling her heartbeat thunder against his cheek, feeling her lungs straining for air.

When she reached for the zipper of his jeans, he froze. "Allison? Are you sure?"

She held his head to her chest. "I've never been more sure, Cole. Never."

There were no more words. Within moments they were out of their clothes. She seemed determined to touch him everywhere with her mouth, her hands, her body. She was like quicksilver in his arms, lightly caressing then darting away, boldly exploring then shyly retreating.

When he shifted so that he knelt between her knees, she looked up at him, her face glowing with expectancy as she pulled him down to her, holding him against her, wrapping her legs around him.

He felt her flinch when he first attempted entry. He started to retreat but she locked her arms and legs around him and lifted her hips, forcing his body past the barrier to sink deep within her.

Cole felt the wonder of being a part of this most precious person for the very first time. She was his own sweet love, and now she was truly his in every way.

She moved with him, imitating his movements, anticipating his wants and needs, loving him until at long last he seemed to burst in a frenzy of pleasure and pain, jubilation and regret, completion and desolation.

For a few moments he'd scaled to the very top of the joys of pleasure. He'd escaped the pain, but only for a moment.

When he came back to reality, his mind was flooded with all that he had momentarily forgotten.

Cole rolled to his side, dragging her clutched to him. The tears flowed, despite everything he could do. He had no more control to draw from.

His deep, racking sobs shook them both as they lay there beside the peaceful creek. She held him tightly, as though sharing his grief in the only way she knew how.

It was almost dusk when Cole felt as though he could finally regain some sort of sanity. He looked at Allison lying in his arms and whispered, "I'm so sorry, baby. I'm so sorry. I never should have—"

She placed her fingers across his lips. "Shh. Don't say it. Don't even think it. We both needed this. We needed today. It's all right."

"But I made a promise that we would wait and now—"

"I know. But things have changed. Everything has changed."

The horrible pain that had been riding in his chest since Aunt Letty's phone call had somehow eased. He could breathe around it now. He could go on.

"Oh, Allison, I love you so much."

"I love you, too."

"You're the best friend I've ever had. I don't think I could have made it without you."

"You never have to make it without me, Cole. I'll always be right here, whenever you come home."

They helped each other to dress, taking their time, pausing to kiss and touch and explore.

"You know, maybe we should plan to get married before I get out of school. I mean, there are lots of married people going to school. You'll be out of high school in May. There's no reason to wait."

She smiled at him. "Let's talk about it during Christmas vacation, okay? Now isn't the time to be making plans."

"But I want you with me, Allison. I need you."

She went up on tiptoe and kissed him lingeringly on his lips. "We'll talk about it at Christmastime."

They rode the gelding back to the house with Allison seated in front of him in the saddle. Nothing had changed, but somehow Cole knew that he had changed. He knew what he intended to do. He and Allison would be married next summer. Nothing was going to change that.

It never occurred to him when he returned to school after burying his parents that he would never see her again.

Three

Cole's mind was caught up in memories of the past while he waited at the hospital for any change in Cameron's condition.

He sat in the shadowed corner of Cameron's room in the intensive-care unit where he could watch Cameron and see all the machines that were monitoring him.

He'd sent Cody home to get some sleep. He doubted that his stubborn brother had followed his instructions. If anything, he would check into a motel close by for some rest. Cole had promised Cody that he would rest as well, but his mind was racing with too many thoughts, too many memories.

Cameron had successfully come out of surgery. Both his left arm and left leg were in casts, and his left leg was in traction. Although the seat belt may have saved his life, there had been internal damage where the strap had held him. The exploratory surgery had taken hours while they

checked for intestinal tearing. They'd had to remove his
spleen as well. There were various tubes in and out of his
body. He lay there totally still. At times Cole couldn't tell
if Cameron's chest was moving at all, his breathing was
so shallow.

"Don't die, Cameron," he whispered. "Hang in there,
buddy. I can't lose you, too. Everyone else in my life
seems to go. Don't you leave me."

He leaned his head against the back of the padded
chair. He wanted someone in the family to be there when
Cameron first regained consciousness. If he was in Cameron's place, he would have plenty of questions when he
surfaced from the drugged oblivion Cameron was pres-
ently in.

He closed his eyes in an effort to ease their stinging.
Mason, Texas. Allison lived in Mason. She and his son
lived within a hundred miles from his Austin home and
he'd never known it.

The boy mentioned something about his grandfather
having died before he was born. How could that be? He
remembered Tony as an active, virile man. Cole had been
furious when Aunt Letty had told him that Tony had resigned as soon as he discovered he'd been named in the
will. He'd told her that he didn't need to work anymore,
that he was clearing out, buying a place in Colorado.

By the time Cole returned home for Christmas that
year, both Tony and Allison were gone.

Had the Callaways meant so little to them that they no
longer cared about the remaining family? How could
Tony have walked away when he knew how much Cole's
dad had always relied on him?

Cole could still feel pain at the thought of their deser-
tion. Was that why Allison wouldn't talk to him about a
wedding that last day they were together? Had she al-

ready known that they would be leaving? Had she decided to dismiss the first eighteen years of her life and never look back?

Her leaving was one more loss that Cole had had to deal with. Now, fifteen years later, he knew that her abandonment had hidden an even worse betrayal...she had been pregnant and hadn't told him.

A slight sound from across the room caused Cole to open his eyes, then spring from his chair. He was at Cameron's side in a couple of steps.

Cameron made a soft moaning sound deep in his throat. His lashes fluttered. Cole took his hand. "I'm here, Cam. You're going to be all right, do you hear me?" His voice was hoarse with emotion. "You're going to make it. I'll be right here with you."

Cameron's eyes slowly opened and he stared at his brother. "Cole?"

"Yes, Cam. It's me."

Cameron closed his eyes once again and didn't stir. After a few moments Cole went out to the nurses' desk. When one of the nurses glanced up, he said, "My brother just spoke my name. He recognized me."

She smiled and stood. "Sounds like great news. Let me go check on him." Cole followed her back into the room. After checking all of Cameron's vital signs, readjusting the drip and the oxygen, she said, "He seems to be resting now. No doubt it helped for him to find you here."

"God, I hope so!"

"Why don't you go get some rest now, Mr. Callaway? You look in worse shape than he does."

He turned away, too choked up to say anything. Cameron was going to be all right. He had spoken to Cole, recognized him. Cam wasn't going to die.

Cole walked down the hallway, unsure about what to do. His answer came when the elevator doors opened and Cody stepped out. "How is he?" were his first words.

Cole grinned. "He came to for just a moment, but he recognized me. He said my name."

"That's great." He reached into his pocket and pulled out a motel key. "Here, we're booked in there for the duration. It's only a few blocks away. Go get something to eat and sleep, for God's sake. You look near death yourself."

"Thanks for the testimonial."

"You know what I mean. You've had two sizable shocks, fella. How about cutting yourself a little slack, okay?"

"Have you spoken with Andrea's parents?"

"Yes. They've made the arrangements for the funeral. It's scheduled for tomorrow. They saw no reason to postpone it."

"That's true. Cameron's not going to be in any shape to attend anything for some time."

Cody rested his hand on Cole's sleeve. "I know the two of you have always been close. It's understandable because you're so much closer in age. But don't forget that I'm here for you. I'll do whatever I can."

Cole nodded. "Thanks, Cody. I appreciate that, more than you know."

"Now get outta here."

"I'm on my way."

The first thing Cole did when he woke up the next morning was to call the hospital and ask for Cody. When his brother came to the phone, Cole asked, "How is he?"

"He's roused a couple of times. He seemed to recognize me the first time, but didn't say anything. The second time he asked for Andrea."

"Yeah, that's going to be a tough one. He needs to be stronger before we tell him."

"That's what the doctor suggested. Guess we'll play it by ear."

"Are you coming back to the motel?"

"Not anytime soon. Why don't you bring me something to eat and some decent coffee?"

"Will do. Have you talked to Aunt Letty?"

"Earlier this morning. The baby is doing fine, of course."

"Poor little one. She's too young to realize what's happened."

"Maybe it's better this way."

"Better or not, this is the way it is. I'll see you in about half an hour."

While Cole showered, shaved and dressed, his thoughts continually returned to Allison. He knew he was going to have to face her again, and he wasn't certain he was in the best frame of mind at the moment.

He wanted to stay by Cameron's side until his brother was able to handle everything on his own.

Cole knew he needed to call the ranch. Dozens of people were no doubt looking for him by now, although he knew that Letty would have told them about Cam.

He was only one person. He couldn't divide himself into enough people to take care of everything that was going on. Business would either keep or it wouldn't. At the moment he didn't care.

Cameron came first.

After he was sure Cameron would be okay he would go find Allison Alvarez. They had some unfinished business that had waited fifteen years too long.

Allison Alvarez heard the bell that signaled someone had come into her gallery from the street on the square. She sighed, knowing that she would have to see who it was since her assistant, Suzanne, had gone a few doors down to the bakery for the best hamburgers ever made. She'd promised to bring Allison one, which was why Allison had relented and let her go.

She was trying to finish the small clay model she'd been working on all week so that it would be ready to be cast in bronze by Monday. She'd faithfully promised the client she'd have it to him on time and she was already running late.

It couldn't be helped. She would—

"Mom? Mom, are you here? Where is everybody? Sue?"

"Tony!" She grabbed a towel and dashed through the beads that served as a divider between the working area of the shop and the gallery itself. "You're home!" she cried, rushing to him and hugging him. "I didn't expect you back until late tonight."

"Yeah, but we decided to get up early this morning and head back."

She looked at her son, still marveling that he was that tiny, red-faced infant that had been placed in her arms what seemed to be such a short time ago. Now he was shooting up so fast she could almost see him grow out of his pants and shoes. He was already several inches taller than she was.

"You're really dark. You must have spent the entire time in the sun."

"Just about."

His black eyes in his tanned face made her think of her father. The difference was the hair. In the summer Tony's hair lightened to an almost honey blond, with streaks of red. Her mother had been a redhead. And, of course, his father had red highlights—but she wouldn't allow her thoughts to go any further.

"Where's Sue?"

"Picking up some hamburgers. Knowing you, you're hungry, right?"

"Starved."

"So go ask her to get some for you, too. Meanwhile, I have to get back to work." She turned away and headed toward the back of the gallery.

She was already pushing the beads aside when Tony said, "Oh, Mom. I almost forgot. You won't believe who I met at the beach. Man, oh man! The guys sure were envious. They saw him but *I* got to *talk* to him."

Her mind already back on her work, she absently smiled at his enthusiasm and asked, "Who?"

"Cole Callaway. He was just walking along the beach..."

His voice faded away to nothing, although she could still see him talking, his arms miming the meeting over the Frisbee, but all Allison heard was a loud buzzing in her ears, a ringing that drowned out all sounds around her. She had to sit. Otherwise she was going to faint. Allison groped her way to her chair and sank into it, burying her head in her lap in an effort to get some blood back into her head.

How in the whole wide state of Texas had Tony managed to run into Cole Callaway?

Nothing in her life had prepared Allison for the shock of Tony's news. They had been in Mason all of Tony's

life. They did not move in the same circles as the Callaways. Tony could have gone his entire life and never laid
eyes on Cole.

Why? Dear God, why?

Tony's voice began to seep into her consciousness once
again. He was still explaining. "So then we got to talking, you know, like what's your name and where are you
from and things like that—"

No! You didn't tell him your name or that we were here
in Mason! No! Please say you didn't!

"I told him about the gallery and all the awards you
won and things. He never did say if the Tony Alvarez he
used to know could have been my grandpa, but it was
neat meetin' him. Really awesome."

So there it was. Cole had discovered exactly what he
had ignored all those years ago. The only question now
was whether he intended to do anything about the information Tony had given him? Tony looked too much like
the Callaways for Cole not to have immediately recognized him. Over the years Allison had sometimes wondered if Cole would grow curious and decide to seek out
the child she had carried, but as the years moved on,
she'd given the matter less and less thought. Tony's news
could not have been more unexpected.

Tony pushed the beads aside in a jangle of soft click-
ing sounds. "Do you think—"

"Tony, I thought you said you were hungry?" she said,
hoping the interruption would distract him.

"Oh, yeah. See ya," he said with a wave of his hand.
In a moment she heard the bell jingle at the front door.

Quiet. Blessed peace and quiet for a few moments
while she attempted to gather her thoughts together. She
looked down at the piece she'd been so meticulously

working on and realized that if she didn't stop right now, she was going to irreparably ruin it.

She got up and walked through to the gallery once again, ending up looking out the large plate-glass window to the courthouse in the middle of the square. Most of the businesses in Mason were directly on the square where the traffic passed through on its way to west Texas or toward Austin in central Texas.

She had stayed in Mason after her dad died because she could think of no other place to go. The people were very similar to the ones she'd grown up with... ranchers, mostly, and she had felt more comfortable there than in San Antonio. A mother at nineteen, her first concern had been for Tony.

Her father had told everybody that her husband had been killed a couple of weeks after their wedding. Poor Dad. Her pregnancy had been the final heartbreak in a series of major catastrophes, all less than a year apart.

The lie about his father was probably the best thing that could have happened for Tony. He'd been raised without the stigma of having an unwed mother. The townspeople had gathered around her when her dad died so suddenly within weeks of her due date. Looking back, she wondered if she could have made it without their emotional support.

Now she wondered if the life she had carefully built here would soon come to an end. If Cole decided to come looking for her, he would have no trouble finding her. Everyone in town knew where she lived, where she worked and what she did in her spare time.

Cole wouldn't even consider the damage he might do to her or to Tony. Now that he had actually met Tony, there was good reason to believe that Cole Callaway would claim what was his. He always had. No doubt he always would.

By the time Tony and Suzanne returned, Tony had already been distracted by food and talk about the rodeo planned for the weekend. He was a natural athlete and he loved to ride. He'd kept every one of his grandfather's trophies and belt buckles from his years of following the rodeo circuit. They were displayed on a bookcase he'd built in his first year of woodworking.

By the time Allison closed the gallery for the day she had a splitting headache and an uncomfortable phone call to make. She was going to have to call one of her customers and explain that she would be delayed in getting his finished sculpture to him.

Tony was already over at a friend's home about ten miles out of town, practicing his riding and his roping. She didn't see much of him these days, with all of his activities, but she refused to hang on to him now that he was growing so rapidly into manhood. Her childhood had been so wonderful . . . with so much freedom and so much to do . . . and Cole Callaway always stood in the center of her memories.

Tony deserved to have a similar carefree time to grow up and learn about life.

She gave up on her headache and went to bed early, praying that the last dose of aspirin would take some of the edge off. She needed to sleep. She needed to forget. Instead, all she could do was remember.

Her name was Allison Alvarez. She lived on the Circle C Ranch with her mommy and daddy. Her daddy was an important man on the ranch. He was the foreman. He was the boss over lots of people. He was the boss over most everybody, 'cept the Callaways. That was the name

of the people who lived in the Big House. That's what the
C stood for on the brand they put on the cattle and the
horses. They put a big C that had a circle around it.

Her best friend was Cole Callaway. He already went to
school. Next year she would go, too. She would ride the
yellow bus that stopped at the end of the lane up by the
highway. Someone always drove Cole up to the highway.
Next year, they would drive her, too.

Cole had a little brother. His name was Cameron. He
was almost two years old. Allison liked to visit the Big
House and play with the baby when Cole's Aunt Letty
wasn't there. Aunt Letty didn't like Allison. She didn't
know why, but she always got angry when she saw Allison in the house. When his Aunt Letty was gone, Cole's
mother would invite her and Cole to come in and play
with the baby. He was so much fun. But better than anything else, Allison liked to be with Cole.

He was strong because he worked around the ranch,
doing things the other guys didn't have time to do.
Sometimes she helped him. Most of the time she tagged
along after him. That was what he called it. Once in a
while he'd tell her to leave him alone, or he'd pull one of
her pigtails, or make faces at her. That hurt so much. She
tried not to cry. She didn't ever want him to see her cry,
but sometimes she couldn't help it.

He taught her everything she knew. He taught her to
throw a ball and to catch it. He taught her to swing a bat.
He taught her how to race him to the barn and back
without stopping.

Cole Callaway was her very best friend.

''Mom, Cole's mother had her baby today. It was another boy.''

''Oh, honey. How wonderful! Is Cole excited?''

"Yeah."

"I know you wish you had a little brother or sister, don't you, darling?"

"Not really. Cole's my brother, or the same as."

"Well, not exactly. He's a Callaway."

"That doesn't matter."

"Maybe not now. But eventually it will make a big difference."

"I don't understand."

"Well, Cole's daddy is a very important man in Texas politics. He's got a great deal of power. Whatever he says goes."

"Does that make him a bad man?"

"Not necessarily. But power can be a very tricky thing, sweetheart. When you're born with it, sometimes you don't even realize when you're using it."

"I don't know what you mean, Mama."

"I know you don't. It doesn't matter. I'm just saying that the Callaways are very rich, very important people. Your dad just works for them."

"But he and Cole's dad are best friends. I've heard them say so."

"So have I. They are very close. That's one of the reasons why your dad decided to stay here and help to run the ranch, so that Cole's dad would have more time to spend in the city. He trusts your dad."

"Like I trust Cole?"

"Like you trust Cole."

"I can trust him like a brother, can't I?"

"Oh, honey, I hope so. I really hope so."

"Oh, Cole, what am I going to do? They told me last night that Mom is really sick and the doctors can't do anything to make her better."

They were sitting on the bank of the stream near their swimming hole. Allison had stayed home from school but could no longer stay in the house and see her mother's pain, knowing there was nothing she could do. She had run to their secret place to be alone. She didn't know how Cole knew where to look for her. She wasn't sure why he'd bothered.

Now he lay on his side with his head propped up on his hand, tossing a small pebble in his other hand.

"I know," he said quietly. "My dad told me about it last night, too."

"What am I going to do? I need my mother. I thought she'd be with me until she got really old. Why does she have to die so soon?"

"I don't know, Allison. I really don't. I can't imagine what life would be like without my parents."

"Me, either," she whispered. "Me, either."

"You've got me, though. Always remember that."

She turned and looked at him, really studied him, so that his fourteen-year-old face was forever etched on her mind: the scattered freckles across the bridge of his nose, the deep blue-green of his eyes, the shock of light brown hair bleached by the sun into variegated colors of gold and honey and silver.

His eyes carried the message in his heart. They were filled with compassion and empathy and understanding. It was that look that caused the tears to flow. He sat up and put his arm awkwardly around her shoulder and laid her head on his bony, narrow chest. He held her and held her and held her until all the tears had been shed and the pain had been acknowledged.

He continued to be right there by her side through the following weeks when her mother's condition quickly worsened. Cole was there when her father came to school to pick her up and to tell her that her mother was gone. It was Cole who stood on the other side of her and her father at the grave site, each one holding her hand. Each one giving her strength.

She would certainly be glad when Cole Callaway graduated from high school and was finally out of her life.

Good riddance!

She was sick to death of hearing about Cole from every girl in senior high school. There wasn't one of them who didn't have a crush on him. They were always trying to make friends with her so she would invite them out to the ranch. But she saw through their silly games. None of them had ever paid attention to her before.

He was too busy these days to know she was alive. He no longer rode the bus. His dad had given him one of the old pickup trucks to drive to school when he was sixteen. He always had to stay after school for ball practice or some meeting.

He got home in time to eat, then he was off every night giving as many of the girls he could see a real thrill. He definitely played the field. Some of the girls didn't have the greatest reputations, either. His parents didn't say much to him. He'd done chores around the place for years. Now Cameron and Cody were doing them. He made good grades so he wasn't wasting his time in school.

He'd forgotten her. Oh, if he passed her in the hall he gave her a cocky grin and waved. Big deal. He was usually walking somebody to class.

What did she care? She'd outgrown him as well. Since she'd started her sophomore year, the boys that had ignored her all her life were now beginning to stop at her locker to talk with her. A few had asked her out, but it was a problem since they couldn't drive and she lived so far out of town.

But it was nice that they asked.

Sometimes her dad let her stay with a girlfriend in town on Friday nights. She always had somebody to ask her to go to the movies with him on those nights. She had a social life. But she was no longer a part of the Callaway lifestyle.

Her mother had warned her. She just hadn't understood. She was the foreman's daughter, that's all, a childhood friend whom Cole had long since outgrown.

When Rodney asked her out she was delighted. He was the same age as Cole, played football and was a real tease. She couldn't believe her luck. He had a car and everything.

The problem was that she didn't really enjoy the evening with him. She couldn't quite put her finger on what bothered her, but it was something in his attitude toward her. Like, he was possessive for no reason. They went for sodas at the regular hangout after the movie and he kept his arm around her shoulders. She kept moving away from him, but he would just laugh and pull her against his side.

His buddies were all making suggestive remarks. One of them had the gall to say, "Better watch it, Rod. You're handling some of Callaway's private stock there." Then they'd all laughed as though she were a big joke. So what if her dad *did* work for the Callaways...that didn't mean they were slaves. She didn't belong to anybody!

When Rodney brought her home, Allison hopped out of the car before he had completely stopped it. "Thanks, Rodney. I had a lovely time." She'd hated every minute of it, but she knew the polite thing to say.

"Say, babe, what's your hurry? Why don't you—"

"I've got to go in. My dad will be worrying."

That's when he'd made his disgusting remark about her and Cole. She'd turned away without saying a word, refusing to let him see how much he'd hurt her. She didn't care what he thought. She didn't care what *any* of them thought!

Rodney left, and from the sound of his tires, he wasn't happy with the ending of the evening. Too bad.

She had deliberately told him to stop by the barn, not wanting to wake up her dad by driving down the lane to her house. She started the long walk to the house when something moved in the shadows.

"Who is it? Who's there?" she demanded.

"It's me."

Cole stepped out of the shadows into the bright moonlight. She couldn't help being startled. She hadn't seen him in weeks, except for occasionally passing in the hallways at school or the lanes at home.

"What are you doing out here?"

"Waiting to talk to you."

"It's late. I've gotta go inside." She began to walk down the lane away from him.

"Allison?"

"What?" she asked while she continued to march away from him.

"I don't want you going with Rod Snyder."

She stopped in her tracks, then slowly turned around. "It is none of your business who I go out with," she said, enunciating each word.

"I'm making it my business."

She turned her back and continued toward the house. The next thing she knew he had grabbed her arm and spun her around to face him. "Don't you ever walk away from me again when I'm talking to you. Do you hear me?''

"Oh, that's right. Mr. Callaway has given his orders. The peons around here are supposed to tug on their forelocks and bow, isn't that the way it goes?''

"What the hell are you talking about?''

"Don't you cuss at me, Cole Callaway!''

"I'm not. I mean, I just want to know what's wrong with you lately. Every time I see you at school you stick your nose up and go sailing past as though there were a bad smell in the air.''

"Well, maybe there is.''

"What's wrong? What have I done? We used to be friends and now you treat me like dirt.''

"*I* treat *you* like dirt? Oh, that's really funny, Cole. You've been so busy with every good-looking girl in school that you never know I'm around.''

He began to laugh. She tried to pull away from him but he still had her arm in a firm grip. "You're jealous," he said, obviously delighted with himself.

"I am not!''

"Of course you are, which is funnier than you know." She tried to twist away from him, but he began to pull her inexorably closer until both of his arms were clamped firmly around her.

She hadn't been this close to Cole in a long time. He'd grown considerably during the past few months. Her head barely came to the top of his shoulder, and his chest had broadened. She had to tilt her face up to see him. When she did he leaned down and kissed her.

This kiss was nothing like she had ever experienced before. It wasn't a slobbery wet kiss like the one Rodney tried to give her, nor was it the shy, tentative kisses offered by her classmates. An experienced male was showing her exactly what kissing was all about. By the time he finally raised his head, Allison's knees were wobbly.

"Allison, honey. I want you to be my girl."

"You do?"

"Yes."

"You mean, like go steady?"

He grinned. "That's exactly what I mean."

She thought her heart was going to burst, it was beating so fast. Cole Callaway wanted her to be his girl. He hadn't forgotten her; he hadn't seen her just as the foreman's daughter. "Oh, Cole." She threw her arms around his neck, effectively pulling him down so that she could kiss him again.

"Whoa, honey. Enough of that for now. I'm only human. We've got a long time ahead of us."

"What do you mean?"

"I've got years of schooling, so do you. We've got plenty of time. I just wanted you to know how I feel about you and how much it's hurt me to have you ignore me for months."

"Oh, Cole, it's hurt me, too. So much."

"So you'll go to the prom with me?"

"The senior prom?" The dream of every sophomore girl, to go to the senior prom.

"Yep."

"Oh, Cole, I'd love to go with you."

"Good. Now go on, get in the house before I do something we'll both live to regret."

Years later, Allison lay in bed, staring up at the ceiling, lost in her memories. His words had been prophetic, after all. They had dated through the summers and during the holidays when he was home from school, but Cole had kept a tight rein on his passion.

He'd taught her a great deal, and she'd learned some heavy-petting techniques. But he had refused to go all the way, insisting that he wanted to wait until they were married.

Only they ended up not waiting. And he had regretted it enough to allow her to get out of his life. He'd made no effort to stay in touch, even after she wrote and told him that she was pregnant. Those months had been even blacker than the time right after her mother had died. Never before had she felt so much shame. She had let her dad down, she'd let herself down.

She had made a vow not to let her unborn child down.

For over fourteen years she had been the very best parent she knew how to be. She had raised Tony with firm values, the same ones her parents had instilled in her. The same values, unfortunately, she had ignored in an effort to comfort Cole when he'd needed someone to love and hold him.

She had to second-guess what the man he was now might decide to do now that he'd come face-to-face with his son for the first time.

She knew from magazines and newspapers that Cole had been involved with many beautiful, socially well-connected women. But he had never married. She often wondered about that. Maybe the thought of marriage had so frightened him at twenty that he had never recovered.

She didn't care what he did. But if he decided that he might like to befriend the child he'd ignored for years, then she would set him straight really fast. He'd made his decision years ago. He would have to continue to live with it.

Four

Cody stopped Cole as soon as he stepped off the elevator. "We need to talk," he said quietly.

"What's wrong? I thought Cameron was doing much better."

"Yeah. They're talking about letting him get out of here soon."

"Then what's the problem?"

"I finally brought up the accident and asked him if he remembered anything about that night."

"And?"

"He said there had been little traffic, but all at once lights flashed directly in his eyes from the middle of the road. He swerved and then felt the impact of something hitting the side of the car, which put it into a spin."

"My God! Is it possible someone actually forced them off the road, causing them to crash?"

"I don't know, but I'd sure like to find out." Cody was quiet for a moment. "There's something else that's been bothering me about Cam's accident."

"What's that?" Cole asked, hardly believing this could be true.

"I know I was just a kid at the time, but I remember when our folks were killed that there was never an explanation for the crash, just speculation. There were no witnesses. If Cam hadn't pulled through, there would have been no witnesses this time, either."

Cole stared at Cody. "Are you saying there could be some connection between the two crashes?"

"I don't know what I'm saying exactly. I just know I have this funny feeling about the similarities. Think about it. No deer were found, there was no traffic and no witnesses. Nobody questioned the accident fifteen years ago. Suppose someone did get away with murder at that time? Whoever it was might feel confident enough to recreate the crime, particularly if he hated the Callaway family enough."

Cole thought about Cody's suggestions and theories. After a few minutes, he mused, "We've never been short of enemies. We've lived with that knowledge all of our lives."

"I know. That's one of the reasons this whole thing has been eating at me. I don't want to sit around waiting for the next so-called accident to take another family member."

"What can we do about it?"

"I've got friends who've got access to records. I want to take a look at the reports filed on the old accident and find out what actually happened the night our folks were killed. I'll be looking for similarities between what happened then and what happened now. Maybe I won't find any connection, but if I do, we need to be warned.''

''Cody, if you're right about this, you could be endangering yourself by asking questions and stirring up more trouble. So be careful.''

''I hear you. If there really is a connection, then whoever's responsible has been incredibly patient to have waited all these years to strike again. We all need to be alerted to the possible danger.''

''Have you said anything to Cam about this?''

''Not yet.''

''Good. He's got enough to deal with at the moment. When you find out anything, let me know.''

''Will do.'' Cody doubled his fist and lightly tapped Cole on the shoulder. ''I'll see you later.''

Cole stood there and watched Cody step onto the elevator and waited while the doors quietly closed between them.

He would call their corporate headquarters and get the security staff to do some research on any other trouble that might have occurred through the years, the origin of which had never been resolved. The more he considered the matter, the more he agreed with Cody. The similarity between the accidents bothered him. He had never believed in coincidences.

Cole walked down the hall with a brisk stride and pushed open the door to the private room that Cameron had been transferred to from ICU a few days before. ''How's it goin'?'' he asked, walking into the hospital room and pausing beside the bed.

''They're talking about letting me out of this place.''

Cole smiled. ''Somehow that doesn't surprise me. They'll probably be thrilled to get rid of you.''

"So that battle-ax of a night nurse informed me. If she thought she was hurting my feelings, she was wrong."

There was an unspoken agreement that no one mentioned Andrea's death. The doctor had broken the news to Cameron when he thought he was strong enough to hear it. Even so, it had set his recovery back. Now, Cole and Cody waited for him to pick the subject for conversation when they visited him. Cole knew that Cam would talk when he was ready, not before. The main thing was that Cameron knew his brothers were there for him, no matter what.

Whatever demons Cameron wrestled with, he fought them alone.

Cole pulled up a chair and sat beside the bed. "How would you like to come back to the ranch to live?"

He'd been dreading having to ask the question, knowing it was going to stir up a great deal of emotion.

"I suppose it makes sense," Cameron responded slowly, "at least at first."

"I was hoping that you'd feel that way. Letty's grown quite attached to Trisha. She'd miss her."

"That really surprises me. I never thought the witch ever cared about anybody."

"Cam! That doesn't sound like you."

"Well, maybe you don't know me, or maybe I've been keeping my thoughts and opinions to myself for too long. There's nothing like almost dying to make you take another look at the way you live."

"What have you got against poor Aunt Letty?"

"Poor Aunt Letty, my rear end. The woman terrorizes everybody around her."

"Where would we be without her, Cameron? You and Cody wouldn't have had anybody if she hadn't been there for you."

"You don't know how lucky you were that you never had to live with her rules and regulations. I swear the woman took pleasure in punishing us whenever we didn't live up to her expectations."

"I had no idea you felt that way."

"I know. I've never told you before. I didn't want to leave Trisha with her at all, but Andrea thought I was being silly. Her parents are definitely not the parenting type. They scarcely knew Andrea was around when she was growing up."

"They asked Letty if they could keep the baby for a while, but she wouldn't let them."

Cameron shifted, as though he were trying to find a more comfortable position. Cole stood and paced over to the window, not sure how to deal with this newly belligerent brother.

"It's just as well," Cameron finally muttered. "They would have turned her over to one of the maids."

Cole turned back to look at his brother. "What did Letty do that was so bad?"

"It wasn't what she did. It was her whole attitude toward everybody. Especially the Alvarezes. God, she was brutal to them, even more so after our folks died."

"Well, Tony's leaving like that left everybody stunned."

"That's what I'm talking about. I don't care what Letty said about their leaving, I don't believe either Tony or Allison wanted to go."

Cole walked over and sat beside the bed once again. "What do you mean?"

"I was there, Cole. You weren't. I saw Tony's face when he came out of dad's old study after talking with Letty. He was devastated, utterly wiped out. He walked right past me like he didn't even see me. Later, when I heard they were leaving, I went over to talk to Allison and Tony. She was crying something fierce. I've never heard worse sobbing."

Cole felt something clutch at his chest, constricting his breathing. "Are you saying that Letty said something to make them leave?"

"I've always suspected it, but I could never prove it. After Tony was gone, she ruled the place like some petty tyrant, ordering all of us about."

"How come I've never seen that side of her?"

"Because you've never paid that much attention to her. She always waited until you had left to pull her shenanigans. Remember, you've spent most of your time in Austin these past few years. You just let the ranch run as it always had."

He was right, Cole knew. There had been so much to learn about all the businesses that he'd bought a place in Austin where he could more easily travel over to Houston or up to Dallas, or down to Corpus Christi. He'd been thrown into the business world like a nonswimmer into the deep end, with very few people there to help keep him afloat.

"Uh, Cameron. There's something that I need to talk to you about, something that's been eating at me. Almost losing you made me face how important you are to me. I don't have very many people in my life I can trust. You're not only my brother, but you're my business consultant, my tax attorney, my friend."

Cameron narrowed his eyes slightly. "Glad to know I'm appreciated. What's up?"

"I recently discovered that more was going on with the Alvarezes than either of us were made aware of at the time."

"What are you talking about?"

"Allison was pregnant when they left."

Cameron sat up in the bed, let out a groan because of the pain his sudden move had caused him and subsided back on his pillow. "She what?"

"The morning after your accident, before Cody found me, I was down at the beach, walking, when I saw a kid that could have been Cody at fourteen. All except for his eyes. They were black, that deep glittery black that always gave Tony and Allison their exotic looks. I stopped and asked him his name. He told me he was Tony Alvarez, and lived with his mother, Allison Alvarez, in Mason, about a hundred miles northwest of here. He said he was named after his grandfather who died before he was born."

"And you think that—"

"I *know* he's my son. There isn't a doubt in my mind."

"God, Cole, what are you going to do?"

"I haven't decided, yet. I've been trying to cope with that knowledge all the time I've been worrying whether I was going to lose you. Now you're telling me that there are some discrepancies in the story about the reasons why the Alvarezes left the Circle C."

"Do you think Letty knew that Allison was pregnant?"

"There's only one way to find out."

"You think she'd tell you the truth?"

That stopped him. Cole stared at his brother. "Are you suggesting that she might lie about it?"

Cameron shrugged. "It wouldn't be the first time she's lied. She always manages to cover up one lie with a bigger one."

"My God, Cam. Surely you're exaggerating. We can't be talking about the same woman."

"The trouble with you, Cole, is that you've always seen what you wanted to see, not necessarily what was happening around you. You've got this thing about family loyalty and family heritage and all that bunk. Since Letty is a Callaway you automatically assume she's an upright, outstanding example of loyalty and compassion."

Cole had gotten sidetracked. "What do you mean, all of that bunk? We *are* a family. We *do* have a heritage. A damn fine one. When Granddad Caleb first came to Texas—"

"Oh, hell, Cole, don't get started on Granddad Caleb. You and Dad always treated him as some saint, of all things. He was nothing but a gunfighter too bored after the First World War to stay home in Ohio. So he came to Texas looking for some action, and he found it. He managed to amass a fortune down here, acquired the ranch in ways that have always been glossed over—"

"He *bought* the ranch, dammit. He didn't steal it. He bought it!"

"Of course he did. For less than a quarter of what it was worth. The owner was glad to get away with his life!"

"Where the hell did you get such stuff?"

"I read, Cole. I've always enjoyed history and, I'll admit, I've especially enjoyed Callaway history. It never ceases to amaze me how respectable we are now considering how all of this got started."

"What did you read?" Cole demanded to know.

"A bunch of letters and journals stored in the attic. While you were busy trailing after Dad all over the ranch I was curled up with some of the juiciest scandals that ever got jotted down by a series of observers—our feminine ancestors."

"And you never told me?"

"Hell, no. I doubt that Dad ever knew it, either. He took *his* dad's word for everything, just like you always did. If Dad said it, you took it for gospel."

"And what's wrong with that?"

"Nothing, except that Dad wasn't a hundred percent right all of the time. He was a human being. He had his faults. But you never saw them. To you, he was your dad and he was perfect. Aunt Letty is the sister of a perfect man and that makes her perfect too. Cody and I are your brothers, making us perfect also."

"I wouldn't go so far as to say that," Cole responded with a grin.

"Then there's hope for you, yet, thank God. I realized while I was telling you about Letty that I felt just like some kind of pervert telling little kids that there's no Santa, no tooth fairy, and that the Easter bunny is a fake."

"I'm not some unsophisticated kid, Cameron."

"You are where your family is concerned. Now you tell me that you have a son, that you've known for—how long?—where he lives but you haven't gone to talk with Allison. Who are you protecting now, Cole? Have you ever, just once in your life, done something that was for you alone, or have you always put the family's needs, desires and reputation before your own?"

Cole discovered that he couldn't answer him. He sat there and stared at his brother, his mind racing. He'd always done what he was supposed to do, what was expected of him. And now, Cameron was saying that was wrong? He was wrong?

"Cole?"

"Yeah."

"Do me a favor."

"Sure. What do you need?"

Cameron smiled. "See what I mean? It wouldn't matter to you what I would have wanted, you would have busted your butt getting it for me."

"Well, sure. I mean, you're my brother and—"

"I know, I know. Well, this request is going to be a tough one for you."

"That's doesn't matter. I can—"

"I want you to leave the hospital and I don't want you to come back."

"What?"

"Let Cody handle getting me home. I'll be able to leave by tomorrow probably, no later than the day after. I want you to forget about me for a few days, okay?"

"But, Cameron—"

"I want you to ask yourself what you would like to do most in the world right now? This is going to be the toughest question you've ever had to face, I'm sure, because you don't have a clue. Not one clue. So take your time. Go home, or wherever you've been staying that allows you to be at the hospital sixteen hours every day. Somehow you've managed to put business concerns aside, so let them stay there for a few more days.

"Decide what you want to do most in the world, Cole. Then go do it. I mean it. That's what I want, and you said you'd do anything. I want you to go do it."

"You don't have any idea what I might do."

Cameron grinned. "Oh, yes I do. But you don't and it's you we're talking about here."

"Well, if you're so all-fired smart, why don't you just tell me and save me all that soul-searching?"

"It's the soul-searching that's so important, bro. That's the part that is crucial, because when you finally face what you truly want, then you'll be ready to go after it."

* * *

Two days later, Cole was on his way to Mason, Texas. After following Cameron's advice and allowing Cody to look after Cameron, he had felt at loose ends.

Cameron's remarks had unnerved him, particularly the ones about Letty. Actually, everything he'd said had shaken him...about Granddad Caleb, about how he'd worshipped his father, about his being blind to what went on around him in the family. How could that be? He'd managed to improve the businesses he'd inherited over the years. He'd doubled, sometimes tripled, the income produced by Callaway Enterprises. He was no dummy. He knew that. But he obviously had a blind spot.

His family.

Tony was part of his family, whether he had known about him or not. When he finally allowed himself to feel all of the feelings that went with the thought of having a son, he was almost brought to his knees. The pain was intense. How could he have had a son all of these years and not known? Shouldn't he have felt something?

As for Allison, he was more confused than ever. He wanted some answers. Most important, he wanted to know why she hadn't bothered to tell him she was pregnant.

Had she told her father? Had he told Letty?

He had considered talking to Letty first, but then Cameron's words had come back to him. Would she tell him the truth?

He knew that Allison would not lie to him. She had never lied about anything in all the years he'd known her...until she chose to live the biggest lie of them all.

Allison was in the gallery visiting with possible customers who had seen her shop on the way through town when she saw the large luxury car turn the corner of the square.

Large, late-model luxury cars drove through Mason on a regular basis, but this one was different, and she knew it with the instincts of a cornered animal.

She watched with a sense of inevitability as it pulled into the angle parking space in front of the gallery.

So he had come.

She turned back to her visitors. "Yes, the work we carry here is done by local artists and craftsmen. Those photographs, the Indian medicine wheels and Kachina dolls, and the oils are the product of various people who live in and around Mason."

The front door gave its distinctive tinkle and she turned.

The years had made a considerable difference in the man. He seemed taller, and considerably broader. He was dressed informally, in a Western shirt, boots and well-worn jeans that clung to his muscular legs. She would have known him anywhere and yet he looked different— harder, somehow. The smile lines were gone from his face. In their place was an austerity in his expression that made him look more somber. His eyes were narrowed and they glittered in the darkness of his face.

"Hello, Cole. It's been a long time."

He hadn't known what to expect, but the woman who stood before him with so much poise and confidence was a far cry from the teenage girl he'd last seen.

She still wore her hair long. Now she had it in a single braid, draped over her shoulder. She was in a multi-tiered full skirt, a matching blouse, doeskin moccasins, and she wore a matching beaded headband. Her skin was still as fair as ever, which made a startling contrast to her black eyes and hair.

"Pocohantas, I presume?" he drawled, slowly scanning her from her toes to the top of her head.

One of the men among the two couples in the gallery laughed.

"May I help you?" she asked Cole, meeting his eyes with a deliberately steady glance.

"Good question. I'll think on it," he replied and began to study the many paintings, photographs and artifacts in the store. She turned away from him and went over to the others.

One of the women said, "Now, honey, don't let us keep you from your work. We're just lookin' at everything."

Allison smiled. "That's what you're supposed to do. Enjoy yourselves. If I can answer any questions, just let me know. I'll be in back."

She turned away, leaving Cole and the other people staring at the contents of the gallery. She walked through the beads and sat at the desk. All right. He was here. The world had not come to an end. She knew that he would follow her, but for now she was determined to keep her head. She was no longer a child. She was a thirty-two-year-old woman who'd managed to raise a fourteen-year-old son on her own. She had a successful career; she was independent. No man was going to intimidate her, not even a Callaway.

She heard the front door and got up to see if she had more visitors.

"Don't bother," she heard Cole say as he pushed the beads aside and stepped into the back room. "It's just your visitors leaving. Do you get many browsers here?"

"Quite a few."

"Doesn't help business much if they don't buy."

"You might be surprised. They'll see something that captures their imagination. Maybe they won't buy it today, but it will nag at them until the next time they happen to be driving through town. Then they come in and buy it."

"What if it's already sold?"

"That's the chance they take, of course. Things change."

"Yes. It's good to see you again, Allison. I tried to picture what you might look like, but it was difficult after all this time."

"You weren't expecting Pocohantas?"

He grinned. "No."

"I dress this way because it's comfortable, because it's colorful and because artists are expected to be a tiny bit eccentric."

"Ah. Your marketing technique."

"Exactly."

"Where's Tony?"

She had been leaning back in her chair during their exchange without offering him a chair. He didn't seem to be bothered and had leaned his shoulder against the door frame and crossed his arms in a negligent pose.

She slowly straightened in her chair at his abrupt change of subject. "Why do you ask?"

"Just wondered."

"He's staying with friends at the moment."

"The same ones he was with on Padre Island?"

"Yes."

"They live around here?"

"Yes."

He sighed and slowly straightened. "So when do you close this place?"

She glanced at her watch. "In about fifteen minutes."

"Good. Is there someplace we could go to talk?"

"There are all kinds of places to talk in Mason," she said with a whimsical smile. "You only have to say it once and by the end of the week everyone knows about it. That's the beauty of a small town. We're a friendly bunch."

"Then let me rephrase my question. Is there someplace we can talk privately?"

She stared at him thoughtfully. If she thought that he would go away if she said no, she'd immediately give him a negative answer. However, she had a hunch that although Cole looked different from the young man she'd known, he was probably as stubborn as he ever was. He'd driven to Mason to talk to her. He wouldn't leave until he'd said his piece.

"My place is private enough," she admitted.

"When will Tony be home?"

That was none of his business. "We'll have time to talk," was all she said.

At five-thirty she flipped the Open sign on the front door to read Closed, pulled the shade on the display window, then looked around at him. "I'm parked in back. I'll drive around in a few minutes." She opened the door and held it for him. He eyed her suspiciously and she smiled. What did he think she was going to do? Make a run for it?

He had no choice but to go through the door. She locked it behind him and walked back through the gallery, turning off the special lighting as she went. When she got to her office area she reached in the drawer for her purse, then let herself out the back door.

She hopped into her Bronco, drove down the alley to the street and turned right. He was sitting in his car, watching for her when she drove past. She tooted her horn. He immediately pulled out and fell in behind her.

She made a left at the corner and headed up the hill. She had a home overlooking the town, near historic Fort Mason. By the time she pulled into the driveway of her modern, brick, ranch-style home, Allison had given herself a stern lecture on not allowing her emotions to sway her tonight.

Cole Callaway may have been the most important person in her life for years, but he was nothing to her now. In fact, he was less than nothing. He had come for his own reasons and would no doubt let her in on them shortly. Until then, she would treat him politely, as she would any visitor. She would treat him like the stranger he now was.

She stopped outside the two-car garage, choosing to leave the truck outside for the moment. She had to get some groceries a little later, anyway. By the time she hopped out of the Bronco, he had gotten out of his car.

"Quite a place you have here," he said, looking around at the quiet residential area and the view of the town in the valley below.

"You can see the clock tower on the courthouse from here."

"Lived up here long?"

"About ten years."

He made no other comment.

She led the way to the front door, which she and Tony seldom used, unlocked the door and pushed it open. She started to step to one side and he waved her through. Rather than argue she walked into the hallway that ran between the front room on one side and the dining room on the other, back to the family room. A sliding glass door opened onto a patio. The view of the west Texas hills was impressive.

"What can I get you to drink? I thought we could sit out on the patio."

"Do you have any beer?"

"I may have." The kitchen was divided from the family room by a kitchen bar, so that Cole watched her walk into that room and open the refrigerator. "You're in luck. There are two in here."

She grabbed a long-necked bottle and set it on the cabinet, then reached for a pitcher and poured what looked like lemonade into a tall glass.

"Do you want a glass for your beer?" she asked.

He grinned. "'Fraid not. Nobody's managed to civilize me quite that much."

The look she gave him was challenging. "I doubt that anyone would even try." She handed him the beer, picked up the glass and walked to the sliding glass door.

The sun was setting, casting the patio area in shade. They sat in comfortable lounge chairs with a small table between them.

"Is this private enough for you?" she asked cheerfully.

"You act as though you've been expecting my visit."

"Why shouldn't I? Tony told me that you and he met. I knew you'd probably show up, out of curiosity, if for no other reason."

He frowned. "You think that's why I'm here? Because I'm curious?"

"I can't think of another reason, offhand. If you have one, I'll be glad to listen."

Cole took a drink in an effort to get his thoughts in order. Whatever attitude he'd expected to run into... anger, rebelliousness, defensiveness, hatred... he'd been certain he could handle it.

But this? He couldn't understand her, not at all.

Finally he said, "I guess I came because I was hoping to get some answers."

She looked at him, puzzled. "Answers about what?"

"Everything. About why you and your dad left the ranch, about why you never told me you were leaving, never told me anything, most especially why you never told me you were pregnant. Can you imagine what a shock it was for me to see Tony, to suddenly discover that I was a father? I need to understand, and I can't. I've lain in bed night after night trying to figure it out. I should never have made love to you that day. I knew that. I never gave a thought to the possible consequences. Not once. But when I left, you knew I was coming back for Christmas. You had my address. Were you so angry at me for taking advantage of you that you didn't think I deserved to know you were pregnant?"

All the time he was speaking Allison stared at him, her puzzlement becoming a frown. When he stopped speaking she was silent for a long moment before she asked, "Are you trying to pretend that you don't know why we left, that you didn't know I was pregnant? Because if you are, I'm really concerned about you, Cole. I mean, that was a traumatic time in your life, the worst possible time, I'm sure. But I can't believe that you just erased everything that happened back then in an effort to forget your pain."

She spoke in a calm, soothing voice that Cole found irritating as hell, as though he'd just escaped from the funny farm and she was trying to mollify him.

He consciously refrained from grinding his teeth, but he could feel a muscle in his jaw jump as a result.

"I haven't forgotten a thing, Allison. Not a damned thing!"

"I disagree with you. But to refresh your memory—my dad and I left within a week after your parents' funeral for the simple reason that your aunt fired him without notice and gave us forty-eight hours to pack up everything we owned and get out."

He stared at her in horror. "You can't mean that."

"I mean it."

"But why? Did she find out—no, of course not. You couldn't have known yourself about—"

"The baby? Oh, wouldn't she have loved to have known that as well! No, there was no way to know then."

"She told me that when your dad inherited the money from my dad's estate, that your dad resigned, saying he was moving to Colorado."

She shook her head. "Your aunt couldn't wait to get us out of there. At the time she fired Dad, we didn't know about the inheritance. Dad had our mail forwarded, otherwise we might never have been notified. The attorneys sent a letter that finally caught up with us."

"In Colorado?"

She stared at him. "No, of course not. We didn't know where to go at first, so we moved to San Antonio. The shock of your dad's death was really rough on my father. I don't think he took in any of it right away—the death, having to leave the ranch. He seemed to be in a daze for several weeks.

"He happened to run into a guy he'd known on the rodeo circuit who furnished the bulls for the bull-riding events. He'd bought a place near here and invited us to visit. We came out for a weekend and Dad ended up accepting a job working on the ranch."

"But according to the will, your dad wouldn't have had to work. He had enough to retire," Cole insisted.

"The letter hadn't caught up with us by then."

She stared off at the hills that lay in deep shadows for a long time before saying, "It was my pregnancy that killed him, though. He'd just about come to terms with losing his job on the ranch. In a way, I think he was relieved not to be reminded of your dad on a daily basis, and neither one of us missed being around your aunt. He'd begun to settle in, he'd even found a small place he was thinking about buying when I had to tell him I was pregnant. He became real quiet after that. Wouldn't talk to anybody. When I started showing and it became obvious that I was pregnant he told folks that I'd only been married a few weeks when my husband was killed and that I had reverted back to my maiden name, not knowing I was pregnant at the time."

She continued to look at the hills, her face averted from Cole. "He used to sit there at night just staring at me with this sorrowful look that cut right through me. I was all he had left and I'd disappointed him. One night he went to bed and just never woke up. I don't think he wanted to live." Her voice had grown softer and softer as she spoke.

"Allison, why didn't you tell me you were pregnant?"

She glanced at him as if surprised to find him there, she had been so lost in her memories.

"Is that the way you choose to remember it, Cole? Is it easier to live with that way? I've always wondered how you justified your behavior to yourself."

"What are you talking about?"

"Look, Cole. It's just you and me here tonight. No one else. You don't have to lie, or defend, or justify a thing. It all happened a long time ago. But don't pretend that you didn't ignore all the letters I wrote to you. I wrote daily at first. Then when you didn't respond, I began to write once a week. Then I told you about the baby. You never bothered to answer a single letter, Cole, which was an answer all of its own.''

Five

———

"What are you talking about, Allison? I never got any letters from you. Don't you remember—you used to hate writing letters. That first year I was away at college, and homesick as hell, I used to plead with you to write me and you sent me a Valentine's card. Period."

Of course he was right that she hadn't liked to write letters. Plus she'd been so busy with school and related activities. It had only been after she'd left the ranch and had been so homesick that she had felt the need to communicate her thoughts and feelings. No wonder he had begged her to write him when he had first gone off to school. It had never occurred to her, until now, how he must have felt that first year away from everything and everyone familiar. She hadn't understood.

"I'm talking about after we left the ranch, Cole. I wrote to you to give you our San Antonio address, then later the post office box number at Mason."

Cole leaned forward, bringing him closer to her. "I never got a single letter from you, do you hear me? Not one. I didn't even know you'd left the ranch until I got home for Christmas vacation. I assumed you had moved to Colorado by then."

She could feel her frustration mount. "We never *lived* in Colorado, I don't care what your crazy aunt said!"

Cole came to his feet. "She isn't crazy!"

She came to her feet as well. "Oh, that's right. She's a Callaway, so that makes her perfect!"

"I never said that."

"You don't have to, Cole. I know how you are about your family. Maybe she isn't certifiable, but she's certainly twisted in her thinking. She hates the world and everybody in it and she always took a particular dislike to my family. Don't pretend you don't remember that, either!"

"I'm not pretending anything, dammit."

She turned away and walked to the edge of the patio, her back to him. "Fine. You're not pretending. You're saying you never heard from me. I'm saying I wrote you at least a dozen letters...the last one telling you that you were going to be a father."

He moved up behind her and placed his hands on her shoulders. "Allison, honey, don't you know that if I had ever, ever gotten a letter with that kind of information in it that I would have been here on the next plane?"

"No," she stated baldly.

"Why not?" He truly sounded bewildered.

"Because I wrote you and wrote you and wrote you and you didn't come."

He turned her around. "Do you think I'm lying to you?"

She stared up at his angry face. His eyes snapped with irritation, but there was no mistaking his sincerity. For the first time, for the very first time, Allison wondered if he could be telling the truth.

What would it mean to the way she viewed the events of her life, particularly during that traumatic time when both of them had lost their parents, if Cole had never gotten her letters?

A sudden rush of feeling swept over her. She recognized it as grief.

She moved her trembling fingers up to her mouth in an unconscious gesture, to suppress the sound of the pain she was beginning to feel. "But how could that be?" she finally whispered.

"How the hell should I know? I don't understand any of this, but I'm going to get to the bottom of it if it's the last thing I do. As far as I knew, when I left you in October, we were going to plan our wedding when I came back during the Christmas holidays. I came home with all kinds of ideas for a wedding and a honeymoon only to find that you and your father had moved, leaving my aunt and my two little brothers alone with a ranch to run. Half of the crew had left by then. Everything was in an uproar. I was going to stay there and manage the ranch but Letty insisted I go back to school, that my education was more important than anything else at that time."

She looked at him with a feeling of horror because his words made so much sense.

"How did you mail those letters?"

She stared at him in confusion. "What?"

"I said," he enunciated slowly, "how did you mail those letters?"

Was he demented? What kind of question was that? "I mailed them the way anyone uses the mail. I put them in the box at the post office."

"You did? You personally put them in the mailbox?"

She thought back for several moments before she said, "Well, I think so. I mean, I would give them to Dad to mail whenever he went to town..." Her voice faded away and there was a long silence between them.

Cole didn't know what to say. How could he accuse her dad of not mailing her letters? What reasons would he have? He and Tony had always been close, hadn't they? Hadn't Tony known how he and Allison felt about each other? I mean, he had never actually sat and discussed his feelings with Tony, or with his own dad, either, for that matter, but both men knew they were seeing each other exclusively. They had been kids back then, with their entire lives stretching ahead of them as though into infinity. They'd had all the time in the world... until the day their world had ended.

Allison feverishly searched her memories. Surely she had personally mailed at least a few of the letters, hadn't she? But that was during the time when her dad had been so upset, when he hadn't known what to do with himself and would take off on long walks in the city.

Had she suggested he mail her letters as a reason to get out? And what about after they moved to Mason? Hadn't he gone into town each morning to meet the other ranchers for coffee? Hadn't it been logical that he take her letters in with him?

"I can't believe this," she finally whispered, her voice sounding ragged.

"Neither can I. None of it makes any sense to me." After another long silence, he asked, "Did your dad leave you a letter or anything, some papers, something?"

She shook her head. ''He'd banked the money he received, allowing it to build up interest while he decided whether to buy a place. When he died so suddenly I didn't know what to do. Tony was born less than a month after Dad died.''

''How did you manage?''

''I'd moved into town by that time and had rented a small house near the post office. The townspeople were wonderful to me. After Tony was old enough to stay with a sitter I started helping a local artist make sculptures. I worked with her for several years until I was able to buy the gallery. I'd won some awards by that time, gotten some recognition and my work began to sell. That's how I was able to buy this place.''

''Then you've made a success of your life here.''

''Yes.'' She'd done it on her own. She'd done it to prove to the Callaways that she could do it. That she hadn't needed them or anyone. She and Tony had managed just fine.

''Allison?''

''Yes.''

''Does Tony know who I am?''

That brought her out of her thoughts in a hurry. She moved away from him. ''No. He knows nothing about the Callaways. He knows I was brought up on a ranch in south Texas, and that we moved to Mason shortly before he was born.''

''But surely he's asked questions about his father.''

''Not for a long time. I told him that his father had been an orphan so there was no family left. He's found several surrogate fathers here who've worked with him and taught him about ranching and rodeos.''

''Rodeos? You mean he's already leaning in that direction?''

"Falling is a better description, but yes. He loves the life."

"Are you going to let me get to know him?"

"That would be a little difficult under the circumstances."

"Dammit, Allison, would you give me a break here? I'm beginning to see that this situation isn't as cut-and-dried as I first thought. We both had some misconceptions about what was really going on, but we're looking at a new perspective here and—"

"I don't care what sort of perspective you're looking at, Cole, I don't want you in my life or in Tony's life. All you'll do is hurt us, and I for one have had all the hurt I want from the Callaways."

"Hurt you! Hell, woman, I loved you! I would *never* have hurt you, you *know* that."

She could no longer see his face and she realized that night had settled on them while they had been talking. She could turn on the patio light, or they could go inside. Even better, she could ask Cole to leave. She could ask, but she had a strong hunch it would do her no good.

The problem was that she didn't think she could take much more of this. Cole was acting like he was the wronged person through all this, which was absolutely outrageous considering what she— Considering that she had been—

Allison sank onto the edge of her chair. "I don't know what to do," she finally admitted out loud.

He followed her and sat beside her. "Well, I suggest that we eat something. I don't know about you, but I haven't eaten since early this morning and I've never been able to think very well on an empty stomach."

"Oh, you're always hungry, Cole. I swear you must be a bottomless pit—" She paused abruptly, suddenly aware that she had fallen back into their old habit of teasing each other, just as though the past fifteen years had never happened. After a moment, she started again. "Come on inside. I'm bound to have something in there to eat."

He followed her into the house and sat at the counter when she walked over to the refrigerator. "Shouldn't Tony be getting home soon?" he asked.

She pulled out part of a ham, some leftover vegetables and a fruit salad. "He won't be home tonight."

"Why?"

She wanted so badly to point out that he had no right to be concerning himself with his son's whereabouts, but she couldn't. How would she feel if she were in his situation? What would she do if she had only recently discovered that she had a child she'd never known existed?

Cole was handling the situation much more calmly than she would have, she was certain. In fact, he was handling it more calmly than the Cole she had known so many years ago.

"The friend he's staying with lives on a ranch where they keep riding stock. They've been practicing every afternoon after school. Since this is Friday, I told Tony he could stay the weekend."

"Oh."

So now he knew.

"What about your plans for the evening?" he asked in a tentative voice.

"What plans?"

"I mean, don't you usually go out on the weekends or something? Have I interfered with something?"

"No, as a matter of fact you haven't. The man I'm seeing is out of town."

"Oh."

They were both silent. Cole wondered what he could say that wouldn't sound as though he were prying.

Finally he cleared his throat and said, "I know this is going to sound strange, but I'd really like us to become friends again."

Allison kept her back turned while she gathered plates, silverware and glasses, then set two places at the bar. She answered without looking at him. "I don't think that would be a good idea."

"Why, for God's sake?"

"Because it wouldn't work, that's why. I would feel that you were watching and judging everything I did and said, trying to decide if I was raising Tony the way you think I should, or—"

"Hey, wait a minute. If I haven't already said it, then you need to know that I think you've done one hell of a job with that boy. He's a delightful kid—warm and friendly and polite. He's not bashful or overly forward. I was very impressed with him. You don't think I'd come in at this late date and try to cause trouble, do you? Hey, Allison, this is me, Cole. You've known me all my life. When did I turn into such an ogre?"

She didn't reply; her expression said it all.

He sighed and ran his hand through his hair. "Oh, I get it. When I didn't answer the mythical letters."

"They weren't mythical. They were very real."

"I know that. I just meant that—oh, hell, I don't know what I meant. I'm just trying to find some basis on which we can establish a new relationship."

"I don't want a new relationship."

"Well, I do, dammit. This is important to me. Family is important to me."

She finished placing the food on the bar, then sat across from him. "Do you think I don't know that?" she asked. "Family is everything to you. But I'm not family. Remember. And Tony is my son."

"Tony is a Callaway."

"Try and prove it."

"All you have to do is to look at him and—"

"That's not legal proof."

He stared at her in shock. "Are you talking about going to court?"

"Aren't you?"

"Of course not. I don't want to create a problem for you."

"Well, you are. Just your coming to Mason creates a problem for me. If Tony finds out you're here he'll have all kinds of questions, like why I've never mentioned you before, like how well do I know you, like why haven't we ever seen you before, like—"

"Okay, okay. But can't we work all of that out? I just want to get to know him. What is wrong with that?"

She didn't want to see the anguish in his eyes, or hear the pain in his voice. She especially didn't want to get caught up in the magic once again of being with Cole. Already she'd made one slip tonight, falling back into their old repartee. What would repeated exposure to him bring to her? Heartbreak, pure and simple. Not to mention what it would do to Tony.

"What do you suggest?" she finally asked him, toying with her food.

"Well." He obviously was taken aback by the question. "School's out in a few weeks. Why don't the two of you come and stay at the ranch for a—"

"Absolutely not."

"Why not?"

"I don't intend to go anywhere near Letty Callaway."

"Oh, Allison, don't be that way."

"I mean it."

"All right. So what if I send her off on a trip some-where? Would you come, then?"

"I don't know."

"Both Cameron and Cody are living there. I didn't tell you, but Cameron and his wife were in a bad accident about the same time I saw Tony. Cameron's wife was killed and he was severely injured."

"Oh, Cole, no! How horrible."

"He has a little girl, Trisha. She's around a year old."

Allison's eyes filled with tears, tears she couldn't shed for her own situation but were permissible for someone else's pain.

"It would give Cameron something to look forward to, if I told him you two were coming."

"I'd have to think about it."

"Do that. You've got some time. I also wish you'd talk to Tony and tell him about me."

Her eyes widened in alarm. "That you're his father?"

"Well, at least tell him that we grew up together. Let him know how important you've always been to me." His steady gaze caused shivers to run up and down her spine.

"If I come, it would be to give you a chance to get to know Tony. It wouldn't have anything to do with me."

"If that's the way you want it."

"That's the way it's got to be."

"How will your boyfriend feel about it?"

She shrugged. "It isn't any of his business. I am my own woman. I don't belong to anyone. I never will."

She made them coffee and afterward, Cole took his leave. She walked him to the door.

"I'd have you tell Tony hello for me, but under the circumstances, that probably isn't a good idea."

"You're right."

GET 4 BOOKS

FREE

Return this card, and we'll send you 4 brand-new Silhouette Desire® novels, absolutely FREE! We'll even pay the postage both ways!

We're making you this offer to introduce you to the benefits of the Silhouette Reader Service™: free home delivery of brand-new romance novels, months before they're available in stores, AND at a saving of 40¢ apiece compared to the cover price!

Accepting these 4 free books places you under no obligation to buy. You may cancel at any time, even just after receiving your free shipment. If you do not cancel, every month, we'll send 6 more Silhouette Desire® novels and bill you just $2.49* apiece—that's all!

Yes! Please send me my 4 free Silhouette Desire® novels, as explained above.

Name

Address   Apt.

City   State   ZIP

225 CIS AGLZ

*Terms and prices subject to change without notice. Sales tax applicable in N.Y. Offer limited to one per household and not valid to current Silhouette Desire® subscribers. All orders subject to approval.
© 1990 Harlequin Enterprises Limited.

PRINTED IN CANADA

Get 4 Books FREE

SEE BACK OF CARD FOR DETAILS

DETACH ALONG DOTTED LINE AND MAIL TODAY! – DETACH ALONG DOTTED LINE AND MAIL TODAY! – DETACH ALONG DOTTED LINE AND MAIL TODAY! – DETACH ALONG DOTTED LINE AND MAIL TODAY!

"I can't tell you how glad I am to have found you after all these years. I feel that I've been given back my youth."

She looked at the self-assured man standing before her, the kingpin who was being touted as the next governor of the state and shook her head.

What a complex man he was. He acted as though finding her and Tony was the most important thing that had happened to him.

"Cole?"

"Yes?"

"Why haven't you ever married?"

"Because there's only one woman I ever wanted to marry, Allison." He touched his forefinger lightly to her cheek. "I'll call you about your visit."

"Don't make definite plans. I haven't really thought it all through."

"I can hope, though, and believe me, there will be plenty of that going on." Before she had a chance to react he leaned down and kissed her full on the mouth. The kiss spoke volumes . . . of his frustration, of his nervousness, of his desire. When he eventually lifted his head he stared into her eyes for the longest time without saying a word.

Then he turned and walked away.

Six

By the time Cole reached San Antonio he felt weak with exhaustion. The tight self-control he'd kept over his emotions had taken its toll. He had another two hours of driving ahead of him before he reached the ranch. He decided to get a room in one of the hotels along the river downtown.

He awoke early the next morning, before the sun had been given an opportunity to do more than brush the city with its golden light. He should reach the ranch in time for breakfast.

His thoughts kept returning to Allison. She'd been a striking young girl. Now she was stunning, her looks even more exotic than he had remembered. She could have made a fortune modeling. Instead she was the one who used models.

He'd been steeled against feeling much of anything when he drove into Mason, but it had taken only one look at her to know he'd been kidding himself.

He had loved this woman with an intensity he'd felt for few people in his life. Being near her again had stirred up all of those reactions within him.

The kiss had been a mistake. Even though he hadn't touched her with anything other than his lips, he'd felt the searing heat spring up between them. It had always been there without their understanding it. Even though he now understood it, he sure as hell didn't have to like it.

His life was complicated enough.

The adobe pillars that marked the ranch's entrance came into view and he began to slow down. They'd had the lane blacktopped a few years ago, which kept the dust under better control. He drove beneath the high wrought-iron arch with the giant *C* circled in its center.

He loved every inch of this place. The mesquite trees, the live oaks, the cacti, the tumbleweeds, the deer, lizards and snakes, the armadillos...the heat, the fleas and the flies. He loved the rolling hills with their outcroppings of limestone and granite. This was his country. He'd been born here. He would die here.

He was home.

The ranch buildings were almost six miles from the main highway. The blacktopped road wound among the hills with an occasional barbed-wire fence running parallel to it. He slowed down when he topped the last rise and surveyed the scene spread out in the bowl-shaped valley below.

The house had been built in the late 1800s by a Mexican don. It was two stories high in front, three stories along the back, with an interior patio filled with a fountain and masses of greenery. The white adobe walls sparkled in the morning sun.

From the distance he could trace the remains of the original exterior wall that had been built to protect against the Indians and outlaws. The arch across the driveway was still there and most of the wall on the entrance side. However, as the ranch had grown and more buildings had been needed, the wall had been removed on both sides and only half of it remained in the rear.

The bunkhouses for the single men were at some distance from the neat row of housing for the married men and their families. He could see a corner of the rooftop of the foreman's house from where he sat.

He accelerated and headed toward the Big House. He had a great deal to take care of today.

When he pulled up in front of the massive front door with its intricate carvings, Cole got out of the car and stretched. The circular driveway directly in front of the Big House was protected from the sun by large shade trees. A breeze rustled the cottonwood leaves, a familiar sound that meant home to him.

He crossed to the front door and went inside. The Spanish tiled floor of the two-storied foyer gleamed, reflecting the light from the end of the hallway that opened directly onto the patio.

He strode down the hallway, glancing into the various empty rooms he passed. He came to an abrupt halt in front of one of the rooms, a sharp pain seeming to hit him in the chest.

Trisha was in her playpen, gleefully throwing out her toys while Rosie, one of the women who worked for his family, laughed and teased her by scooping them up and tossing them back inside.

Here was a stage of Tony's life that he had missed. This domestic scene brought home to him—more than anything else that had happened—how much he had been deprived.

He paused in the doorway, then slowly walked into the room. "Hello, little girl. Do you have a hug for your Uncle Cole?"

Trisha glanced around and when she saw him she started bouncing on her bottom, holding her arms up.

"Uh-huh, just as I thought." He leaned over and picked her up. She began to finger his collar and play with one of the buttons. He nuzzled her neck, smelling her powder-scented skin, feeling its softness, and for a brief moment he wanted to cry out at the injustice.

Trisha babbled to him in her special language, pulling his nose with one hand and patting his cheek with the other.

"You're a beauty, did you know that, sugar?" he said with a wistful smile. "You're going to be a real heart-breaker someday."

Reluctantly he put her back into the playpen where she immediately picked up a rubber giraffe and threw it at him. "You're also going to be a hell of a pitcher, with an arm like that," he added, chuckling.

He turned and went back out into the hallway. He decided to look upstairs to see if Cameron was settled in. He passed three doors in the upper hallway before pausing in front of the fourth and quietly opening it. Cameron was on the bed, staring out the window.

"Care for some company?" Cole asked softly.

His brother looked around. "Why not? There's not much else to do. I called the office this morning and was told you'd left orders not to send me any of my files."

Cole smiled. "You didn't think I'd know what your first request would be?"

Cameron shifted restlessly. "It would at least give me something else to think about. I feel so helpless at the moment."

"I understand the doctor intends to put on a walking cast in another ten days or so. That will give you some freedom."

"Did you talk to Allison?"

Cole wandered over to the window and looked out. "Yeah, I talked to her."

"Did you get any answers?"

"None that I liked."

"You didn't expect any of those, did you?"

Cole shrugged. "Guess not."

"Tell me."

He turned away and walked over to the easy chair that sat near the immense four-poster bed. "You've got enough on your mind without adding my problems."

"Which explains exactly why I ask. I'd rather think about yours for a change."

Cole gave his brother a half smile. "I can see your point." He sank into the chair and leaned back, propping his feet on the side of the bed. "Allison told me her dad was fired and given forty-eight hours to get off the premises."

"Good God, Cole! I was right."

"Seems that way. Plus, she said that she wrote me several letters, at least a dozen. When I never responded she gave up."

"Letters you never got, I presume?"

"Right. This was the first time it ever occurred to me that she might have written. She was a lousy correspondent."

"What happened to the letters?"

"We'll probably never know for certain. She recalls giving them to her dad to mail."

"But that makes no sense! Why would he not mail them?"

"Who knows? He was upset over losing his job and having to move. He died a few months afterwards. Who knows what was going through his mind?"

"Are you going to talk to Letty?"

"You're damned right I am. I've asked Allison to come to the ranch for a visit when school's out."

"And she said?"

"Not if Letty's around."

"And you said?"

"I'll take care of Letty."

Cameron laughed. "The hell you did! Good for you, old man."

"Have you talked to Cody?"

"About?"

"He was going to check to see if he could find out anything more about your accident."

"No, we haven't discussed it. No doubt it was some drunk who probably doesn't even remember that night. The sooner we all put it behind us, the better off we'll be."

"I suppose you're right," Cole conceded slowly, not wanting to bring up his suspicions at the moment. "Do you know where Cody is?"

Cameron rolled his eyes. "Cody is a law unto himself and you know it. He keeps his own hours. He does his own thing."

Cole sighed, silently agreeing with Cameron's assessment. "I feel that I'm letting him down. He's always been something of a loner and I didn't attempt to get closer to him. I buried myself in my work.''

''We both did.''

''But if Letty treated him the same way she treated you—''

''You have to hand it to her in one respect, Cole. The woman's consistent.''

''I need to talk to Cody about it.''

''Good luck. Maybe you'll be more successful than I've been in the past. He's always kept his own counsel with me. But then you've always been his hero, so maybe he'll open up to you.''

''What's this hero business?''

Although he smiled, Cameron's eyes were bleak. ''You're an easy man to idolize—every fibre of your being is heroic material.''

''That's bull—''

''And modest besides. How can any woman resist you?''

Cole straightened in his chair. ''Man, you're getting more ornery with each day. I'll be glad when they let you up.''

''I'll be glad when you let me get back to some of my work.''

''All right, you win. I'll call and tell them to let you have anything you want. The worst that can happen is that you'll end up in bed again.'' He came to his feet and stood beside the bed. ''Hang in there, buddy. You've almost got this thing licked.''

''Sure I do.''

''Have you seen Trisha this morning?''

The flash of pain that suddenly appeared on Cameron's face at his words caught Cole off guard.

"I, uh, no, I haven't. I'm not ready to face her just yet. She's such a reminder of . . ." His voice trailed off.

"I can't tell you what to do, Cam, but I think you're making a mistake. Just be thankful you have her and that you've been given the opportunity to be with her every day of her life."

Cameron's eyes registered his understanding of Cole's meaning. "I know what you're saying and I know you're right, but every time I see Trisha, all I can think about is Andrea." His voice roughened during the last few words.

"Do what you have to do," Cole said softly. "I understand."

He left Cameron's room, and went looking for Letty. When he found her she was out in her vegetable garden, criticizing one of the hired hands for some dereliction of her instructions.

Letitia Callaway was of average height and in the past few years had added some weight to her gaunt frame. She wore her hair, a heavy mixture of gray and brown, pulled tightly back from her face into a bun. Her face might have been pretty at one time, but years of frowning and irritableness had made their indelible mark.

"When you're through there, Letty," he said, pitching his voice so that she would hear it from where he stood at one of the rear entrances, "I'd like to have a word with you."

"What is it now, Cole? Can't you see I'm busy?"

"I can see that you're keeping that man from doing his job. Why don't you let him do it without your help?"

She spun on her heel and marched toward him. She wore her usual jeans and shirt and boots, as though she were ready to go horseback riding at any time. Cole couldn't remember ever having seen her on a horse.

"He's not doing what he was told," she exclaimed as she came up to stand beside Cole.

"Alfredo has managed to keep us with fresh vegetables for more years than I can remember, Letty. I doubt that he needs your advice."

"But I told him that—"

"Come in and have a glass of iced tea. I want to talk to you."

"So you said. I don't know what's so all-fired important that it can't wait. What are you doing here, anyway? Cody said you probably wouldn't be here for another week or more. What's going on in Austin? Have those idiots made up their minds yet what they want? I can't believe—"

"Letty?"

"What?"

"Let's allow the politicians to run the government without our help for a moment, all right?"

She sniffed, then turned away and started for the kitchen, her back stiff.

Cole shook his head. What made a woman turn out to be so filled with resentment, so bitter about so much? He wished he knew. She'd been this way for as long as he could remember. Not that he'd ever let her disposition bother him. He'd adopted his dad's attitude toward her, tuning her out most of the time, tolerating her the rest.

He followed her into the kitchen. She had two large glasses filled with ice and was pouring their tea while Angie, the family cook, worked across the room chopping up vegetables.

"How's it going, Angie?" Cole said.

She glanced around and when she saw who it was, she gave him a brilliant smile. "Why, I didn't know you were here, Cole! Are you looking for some of my fresh baked cookies?'' Before he could answer, she reached over and pulled out a handful from the cookie jar and put them on a small plate.

"Thank you most kindly, Angie. You sure do know how to treat a man."

He heard Letty snort in the background. Angie handed him a tray. He reached around Letty and picked up the two glasses, added the plate of cookies to the tray and started out of the kitchen.

"Where do you think you're going with that?" Letty demanded.

Without breaking his stride, Cole called back over his shoulder. "I know where I'm going with it, Letty. Into the study."

By the time she caught up with him he'd sprawled himself in the big chair behind the desk and put his boots on its shining surface.

"Cole! Get your feet off the furniture. That's no way to sit. My gosh—"

"Enough, Letty," he said, reaching for a cookie. "Sit down. We need to talk."

She marched over and sat on the edge of the chair in front of the desk, her spine rigid. "All right, then talk."

"I want to know about Tony Alvarez."

She froze, staring at him as though he'd used a particularly obscene phrase. "I beg your pardon?"

"You heard me."

"What in the world is this all about?"

"I want you to tell me about Tony Alvarez." He said it clearly and with precision.

"I have nothing to say on the subject."

"Letty, you have run this place for the past fifteen years with an iron fist in an iron glove. Unfortunately I've allowed it. I can make excuses for my behavior—I was young, grief-stricken, overwhelmed by new responsibilities, attempting to get an education, trying not to fail in my duties...you name it. What I want to hear from you is how do you explain your behavior during this time?''

She started to get up and he gave her a level stare that seemed to freeze her in place, halfway out of the chair. Slowly she lowered herself. In a voice that he hadn't heard in years, she asked, ''What's wrong, Cole? What's upset you? Tell me about it.''

He heard the traces of the warm, compassionate woman she must once have been, but only traces. Her face showed almost no expression.

''We're not talking about me, Letty,'' he said, ignoring her gambit. ''I want to know about you.''

She held his gaze for several minutes in silence before she finally dropped her eyes to her lap.

''Why, Letty? Why did you fire Tony Alvarez?''

Her head jerked upward. ''I never—''

He held his hand up as though halting traffic. It had the same effect on Letty. ''I want to know the truth, Letty. I've listened to your lies for years. It's time for the truth.''

''I don't know what you're—''

''Letty...'' The warning in his voice stopped her exhortations of innocence. ''The day after the funerals—'' neither one of them needed to be reminded of the funerals he referred to ''—you called Tony Alvarez into this office and you fired him. You told him he had forty-eight hours to leave the ranch. I want to know why.''

She lifted her chin slightly. ''What difference does it make? All of that happened years ago.''

"I want to know why, Letty. We will sit here until I get the information I want from you. So it's your choice how long we sit here and play this out."

"Tony Alvarez was trash. He was never any good. I could never understand what Grant saw in him in the first place."

Cole reached for a cigarette and carefully lighted it before he said, "For your information, Tony Alvarez was the only reason that Dad made it back from Korea. He'd been wounded and left for dead. Tony went back and got him. He managed to carry Dad to safety."

"Ha! Is that what Tony told you?"

"No. That's what Dad told me. Tony was given a Medal of Honor for his heroic act, but nobody ever heard about it around here. He made Dad promise not to mention it."

"So why did he?"

"Because I was asking about Tony one day and Dad told me that if it hadn't been for Tony, none of us—me, Cameron or Cody—would have been here. That we would never have been born."

"That sounds like Grant. He was always so dramatic."

"He wasn't the only one with a flair for drama, Letty. You've certainly provided enough scenes over the years to have won several awards."

She stared at Cole in astonishment. "Cole! I've never seen you like this before. You've always treated me with love and respect. What is the matter with you? Has this affair with Cameron been too much for you? I don't—"

"So you decided to get rid of Tony and Allison as soon as Dad was gone. What was it, a chance to flex your newfound power over three young boys?"

"We didn't need him around."

"On the contrary. By the time I got home for Christmas, the place was in total chaos."

"We survived, didn't we?"

"This isn't about survival, Letty. I want to know what you had against Tony that you couldn't wait to get rid of him."

"I told you. He was trash . . . an opportunist. He always played his cards for the main chance . . . flirting and smiling, flashing those black eyes as though he were God's gift to all womankind."

"What rot! Tony was totally devoted to Kathleen and Allison. I've never known a more devoted family man."

"Oh, sure, by the time you came along, he'd settled down. You don't know what he was like before he married. He was wild. He was—"

"You were in love with him, weren't you?" Cole said quietly, with sudden insight and, at long last, understanding.

"Don't be ridiculous! He might have saved Grant's life but he was a nothing, a nobody. How he could even think that a Callaway would look twice at him, would actually be interested in his advances, would be willing to forget her upbringing! Why, it was out of the question, completely absurd. And so I told him."

He could see that his remark had hit home. Red blotches appeared on her face and neck as she talked, showing more and more agitation.

"When did you tell him that?"

"The afternoon we went out riding, of course. He'd suggested we stop and rest awhile, cool off at the stream. Well, I *was* warm. It had been a beastly hot day. Perhaps I should have made it clear to him that I was not with him for any reason other than wanting to get away from the house for a few hours. I had no idea he'd see my going with him as encouragement. I was young. Too young. Ignorant about men. Nobody had ever paid any attention to me before. I knew I wasn't attractive. It didn't matter. When he kissed me I didn't know what to do. I was flustered. Then he kept on kissing me and kissing me. It was horrible!''

"Horrible?"

"The way he made me feel, like some wanton who cared nothing about herself or her reputation. Who only wanted a man to—to—" Her words began to slow down and she realized what she was saying. She stared at Cole in horror at her loss of control.

"So he seduced you?"

"No! But he told me a bunch of nonsense about loving me and wanting to marry me. Lies. They were all lies and I knew it. I laughed at him. Told him he was a fool to even consider that a Callaway would marry him. He was nothing—less than nothing. I remounted my horse and rode home. I learned my lesson well that day. I've never been on a horse since. I'll not be tempted by the earthiness of riding a sweating horse. I hated it. Just as I hated Tony Alvarez!''

Cole studied the woman across from him, seeing her as though for the first time. Letty Callaway—a person so filled with ridiculous pride that she had forbidden herself the most simple of pleasures—the joys that can be shared between a man and a woman. Instead she had become a twisted caricature of an old maid, taking out her anger and resentment on all those around her.

How could he not have seen her for who she really was? How could he have allowed this woman to care for his brothers at the impressionable ages of ten and fifteen?

She had fired Tony Alvarez because he was a constant reminder of her own sensual nature. He knew now that she would never tell him what she told Tony that day. Perhaps she had only told him to get out, without giving a reason. So he had left, grief-stricken, mourning not only the loss of his best friend but of the life he'd established there on the ranch.

What must he have felt when Allison had told him she was pregnant? It wasn't the pregnancy he must have been ashamed of, but the fact that his grandchild would be a Callaway. Of course he hadn't wanted Allison to have any contact with Cole. He probably thought that Cole was enough like Letty to merely laugh at the idea of marrying an Alvarez.

Dear God! What a mess.

Letty sat watching him with a hint of uncertainty. When she saw that he was aware of her once again, she said, "Don't you see, Cole? It doesn't matter anymore. All of that happened so long ago. None of it matters."

"You think not? Then let me disabuse you of your misconception, Letty. When Allison Alvarez left the Circle C, she and I were unaware of the fact that she was carrying my baby."

Letty gasped. All color left her face. She sat there staring at him, her horror almost tangible.

"Because of your hatred, because of your stupid, silly pride, because of your ridiculous belief that being a Callaway meant anything at all, you deprived me of my son for the past fourteen years."

"Oh, no, Cole," she whispered, her hands clenched together and pressed against her mouth.

"I only found out a few weeks ago that I had a son and that he lives within a few hours of me. Yesterday I went to see Allison and we talked about what had happened and why. The day you told him to leave, you succeeded in killing Tony Alvarez as surely as if you had shot him. It took him less than a year to die after that.''

She let out an anguished cry, but he ignored her.

''The irony is that my son is also named Tony Alvarez—the son who should have been brought up on this ranch, the son who will someday inherit all that I have, carries the name of the man you scorned and turned away from here.''

Tears streamed down her face. ''Oh, Cole, I didn't know. How could I have known? I would never have— You know I couldn't have possibly sent them away if I'd known!''

''Letty, after what I have learned these past few days, there isn't anything that you could do that would surprise me.'' He studied her for a moment in silence. She looked as though she'd aged ten years. Her rigid spine was now bowed, her head, which she had always held like royalty, was bent.

She had to live with what she had done, just as he did. The difference was, he had never been given a choice.

Cole stood and walked over to the door. Just before he opened it, he said, ''I've invited Allison and Tony to visit the ranch as soon as school is out. I would prefer that you take a nice long trip somewhere, preferably out of the state or even the country. I don't care where you go, I'll pay for it. I just want you away from here for the summer. Come September we'll talk about this, when we've both had more time to think about the situation. I want my son. I don't know if Allison will ever be able to forgive me for allowing you the freedom to send them away. I'm not sure I'll ever be able to forgive myself. You see, I've trusted you because you were family. As a result, you deprived me of the family I've always wanted.''

Cole opened the door and walked into the hallway, quietly closing the door behind him. Then he went out to the barn and saddled one of the horses. If there was any peace to be found, he knew he would find it in the hills.

Seven

——

"Mom?"

"Yes, sweetheart."

"Is something wrong?"

Allison looked up at Tony seated across the kitchen bar from her. "No, of course not, why?"

"I dunno. You just haven't said much since I got home. Are things all right at the shop?"

"Everything's fine. Sorry I've been distracted."

"Guess you miss Ed, huh?" he offered tentatively.

"Who?"

His eyes widened. "Ed, Mom. You've been seeing him for over a year now! Whadaya mean, who?"

Allison could feel the heat fill her face and knew that the color had betrayed her. She knew she was going to have to explain, but she wasn't sure how much to say, or what to say, for that matter. She wasn't surprised that

Tony noticed her preoccupation. They were both highly tuned to each other's moods.

"Guess who came into the shop Friday afternoon?" she asked brightly.

He eyed her with suspicion. Apparently her cheerful tone hadn't fooled him, either. "Who?"

"Cole Callaway."

He dropped his fork into his spaghetti and stared at her in shock. "You mean *the* Cole Callaway? The one I met on Padre? The one—"

"Yes, Tony. That Cole Callaway."

"Wow! He actually came to Mason! Why didn't you call me? We could have come into town and seen him. Maybe we could have gone to dinner or something. Or maybe—"

"He couldn't stay long," she told him. "He was just passing through, but when he saw the gallery on the square he remembered running in to you, so he stopped in to say hello."

"You mean you know him?"

"Yes, I know him."

"And you never told me?"

"It never occurred to me to mention it to you, Tony. I wasn't aware you knew who he was."

"I didn't until last fall," he said matter-of-factly. "We studied him in current events when he was in all the papers about trying to get a legislative bill passed regarding offshore drilling rights. I had to do a bunch of research and give a report on him."

It was Allison's turn to stare at him in astonishment, struck by the irony of the situation. "Why didn't you tell me?"

He gave her a superior smirk and repeated, "It never occurred to me to mention it to you," he said in a sweetly falsetto voice. "I wasn't aware you knew who he was."

"Touché," she murmured, as the shaft went home.

"So how do you know him?" he asked after another bite of food.

She gave a quick prayer requesting immediate assistance and said, "Well, actually, we grew up together."

"You did?"

"Uh-huh. Your grandfather was foreman of his father's ranch."

"Then it *was* Granddad—the Tony Alvarez he knew."

"Yes."

"Wow. That's totally awesome."

She tried to sound as casual as possible when she said, "He asked if we'd like to come to visit him at his ranch as soon as school is out."

"Are you serious?" he asked, skeptically.

"As a heart attack," she responded gravely.

"Mom!" he shouted, leaping from his chair. "You really mean it! He wants us to go see him? He wants us to actually visit his home? He wants—" He stopped in mid-hop and stared at her. "Why?" he suspiciously demanded to know.

She took a deep breath, exhaled and smiled at her son. "Well, because we managed to lose contact with each other over the years. He thought it providential that he ran into you like that, and found out where we lived. He thought it would give us a chance to catch up on what's been happening with each other and give you a chance to see where I grew up."

"I thought you grew up in San Antonio."

"Well, we lived there for a while."

"How come you've never told me about growing up on a ranch before?"

She shrugged. "Because I was trying to put the past behind me. There were many very painful things that happened to me back then. I didn't need the reminder by discussing my childhood."

He sank back into his chair and nodded. "Oh, yeah. First your mom died, then my dad died, then my grand-dad died. I guess that was pretty rough on you, wasn't it?"

She looked down at her plate, where she had wound spaghetti around the tines of her fork as well as around the handle of her fork. "Yes . . . yes, it was."

"So are we going to go?"

"If you'd like."

"You bet I would. When do we leave?"

"We haven't made any of the final arrangements. He said he would call in a few days and we'd discuss them."

"Well, when he calls, can I talk to him?"

"If you're here, of course you can."

As it turned out, though, Cole called the gallery the following Friday, while Tony was still at school. As soon as she heard his deep voice she knew who it was.

"Sorry I haven't been able to get back with you sooner," he said, once he'd unnecessarily identified himself, "I had several things to take care of that took more time than I thought."

"No problem. We never specified a time."

"True, but I was eager to get back with you to see if you'd given the matter any more consideration."

"I've more than considered it . . . I mentioned the invitation to Tony. Now the whole idea is out of my hands. He's been packed, ready to go, since five minutes after I told him you'd come to visit."

There was a silence that made her wonder if he was taken aback by her remarks. When he spoke, she realized that she was right. He hadn't expected her to be so open to the idea of returning to the ranch, even for a visit.

"How, uh, did he take it? I mean, about my visit...the reason for it."

"I didn't tell him. I haven't decided what to do about that aspect of the situation. He thinks his father is dead. For the time being, I see no reason to upset him with another explanation."

"I see."

There was another long pause.

"Look, Cole. I know this is hard for you. It isn't easy for me, either. Learning that you never got my letters has been quite a shock for me. It's taken time for me to adjust to the idea that you've never known. I mean, for years I assumed that you didn't care, and now to find out that—well, it's just hard to readjust years of thinking something happened a certain way, then discovering it didn't."

"I'm in the same place, Allison, believe me. I've lain awake nights thinking about the things I could have done. I could have hired somebody to find you. I could have insisted Letty tell me where you'd gone. I guess what I've discovered is that regrets are the most useless waste of energy known to man."

"I know."

"The thing is, I'd like to put all of that behind us, if you think you can. I'd like to begin again. I just met this very attractive widow with a fourteen-year-old boy. I'd like to get to know them both a great deal better."

Allison's heart leaped in her chest and began to race in reaction to his remark. "Uh, Cole, I, uh, don't think that's a good idea." She rushed into an explanation. "I mean, I can understand that you want to get to know Tony. That's only natural. And I know he's going to want to get to know you. Would you believe that he did a report on you last fall for his current-events class? That's positively eerie when you think about it. But as for me, well, that's behind us now and besides, I'm seeing Ed and it wouldn't be right if—''

''Ed? Who's Ed?''

She smiled at the irritation in his voice. ''He's the fellow I've been seeing for the past year. You remember, I mentioned that he was out of town last week.''

''You mean you and this Ed are serious?''

No, she wanted to say. But Ed was safe. She was comfortable with him. He was undemanding, appreciating her companionship when he was in town, which was usually only once a month or so. But did she want Cole to know that?

''All I'm saying is that you and I were friends a long time ago. Let's see if we can continue that friendship without any complications, okay?''

Cole clinched his teeth in an effort not to say what immediately came to mind. No, it wasn't okay. Of course he wanted a friendship with her, but he wanted a hell of a lot more than that. He'd been cheated the first time around, but this time he intended to fight for what he wanted.

''Sure, Allison,'' he said instead. ''Whatever you say.''

He heard her sigh of relief. ''Thanks for being so understanding, Cole. I really appreciate it.''

''No problem. Oh, by the way, I drove Letty to Austin today. She and a friend decided to tour Europe this summer. They plan to take a couple of cruises through the Scottish Isles and along the Riviera. So you'll be visiting the Callaway brothers as we 'bach' it here on the ranch.''

''How is Cameron?''

"Improving. Cross as a bear. I think seeing you would really cheer him up."

"You think so?" she asked, intrigued.

"I know so." But don't even think of volunteering to nurse him through this bad time in his life!

Eventually they got around to discussing when school let out and when they could get away. Allison had already arranged with Suzanne to run the gallery while she was gone. By the time they hung up, Allison had agreed to allow Cole to come to Mason to pick them up.

Cole smiled with satisfaction as he moved away from the phone. Though he knew that he would have to work eighteen-hour days for the next few weeks in order to spend some time at the ranch the first part of June, he didn't care. He'd do whatever he had to do in order to have Allison back at the Circle C.

She'd always been stubborn. It was part of her charm. He had a definite advantage over this Ed character. He knew her so well. He knew what made her tick. He knew what could set her off.

He could only hope that somewhere, deeply buried within her, she still loved him. That hope would fuel his resolve during the next hectic weeks.

Allison elected to sit in the back seat of the luxury car so that Tony and Cole could visit. Cole had carefully hidden his smile when she first suggested the seating arrangements, blandly agreeing to whatever the two of them wished to do.

They hadn't been on the road half an hour before Cole realized that he might have been a little too smug. Tony Alvarez had a sharp mind that he continued to hone with a startling array of insightful questions.

"How long have you known my mom?" he asked, starting off innocuously enough.

Cole glanced through his aviator shades into the rearview mirror. Allison was turning the pages of a magazine, seemingly oblivious to the conversation in the front seat. Fine with him. He would be delighted to give his son as many details as requested.

"Since she was born, although I don't remember that particular time in our relationship," he said, eyeing the back seat in hopes of a reaction. "I was only two and a half at the time. The first memory I have of your mother was her following me everywhere I went, like an eager puppy."

Tony laughed. "I would've liked to've seen that!"

"She was a good sport, though, I'll have to admit. From the time I could dress myself I always had chores to do around the place. Allison would be right there helping me."

Tony glanced over his shoulder. "No wonder she's so big on my doing chores. She probably thinks they build character or something." Only a hint of disgust betrayed his attitude on the subject.

"Probably," Cole agreed without giving way to a smile.

"So how come the two of you lost touch with each other, if you're such good friends?"

Ouch. The kid had unerringly gone to the touchiest button and leaned on it with nonchalant skill.

Once again Cole looked into the rearview mirror. This time Allison was looking at him, waiting to see what he would say. It would serve her right if Cole told him the truth, but he knew that now wasn't the time to hit Tony with a full view of the past. He wouldn't do that to him, no matter how much he ached to get beneath Allison's guard.

"Several things happened at about the same time that were traumatic for both of us. You have to remember that we weren't much older than you are now." He heard the words and felt the emotional impact of them at the same time. My God! Allison had only been a little more than three years older than Tony when she got pregnant! She'd been a mere baby! "I was going to college back East when my folks were in an automobile accident. They were both killed."

"Gee, that's too bad. I'm really sorry."

"Thanks. Nobody's ready to lose their folks, but especially not in such a sudden, brutal fashion." He was quiet for a moment, remembering. "I was really wrapped up in my own grief at the time. It was only later that I discovered your mom and grandfather had moved away from the ranch. I never heard from them again."

"Did you know my dad?"

"Your dad?" he croaked, then cleared his throat.

"Yeah. Mom never talks about him much. I guess it must be really painful for her, even after all this time. Sometimes I wonder if I remind her of him or something. She'll look at me once in a while and get this really funny expression on her face, like she's remembering something . . . or somebody. I used to ask her about him a lot when I was younger but I could tell it upset her whenever I brought him up, so I just stopped asking."

"Well, uh, I don't remember him," he finally said. "She must have met him after they moved away."

"Oh. I guess it really doesn't matter. I mean, I'm sorry he died and all, but I'm just glad he was around then. Otherwise I wouldn't be here!"

"That's true."

"The way I figure it, it isn't as important where you came from if you know where you're headed."

"Sounds like a sound philosophy to me. I take it you know where you're going?"

"I hope so. Mom insists I go to college and I guess she's right, but what I really intend to do is work the rodeo circuit for a few years, like my granddad. Boy! You should see the trophies and things he won. I figure with the prize money I'll make I'll save enough to buy a ranch."

"Is that what you want to be, a rancher?"

Tony grinned. "I know, you're going to tell me that you can't make any money being a rancher. I've heard all those stories all my life. But I notice that everybody who tells me that is real content to remain a rancher!"

"The thing to do is to diversify."

Tony looked at him, puzzled. "What's that mean?"

"That means that you do a little ranching, invest in some real estate, maybe get into the oil business, or find a little business somewhere, or—"

"Oh! You mean like you did. But then, you already had a lot of that stuff in your family, didn't you? I mean, you didn't have to go out and do it all on your own."

Nothing like a fourteen-year-old to cut you off at the knees! "That's true. But I've made our businesses even more profitable, improved our strain of cattle—"

"Got laws passed to help your oil business," Tony added helpfully.

Cole's eyes cut to the boy sitting beside him watching the scenery roll by. What the hell did the kid breakfast on, anyway, the *Wall Street Journal?* He glanced into the mirror. All he saw was the top of Allison's head as she continued reading the magazine.

"Are you hungry?" he asked in a desperate attempt to change the subject.

Tony grinned. "I'm always hungry. Mom calls me the bottomless pit."

"We can stop up here for something to eat, if that's all right with you. They make the best smoked ribs I've ever eaten. Their barbecue sauce is a highly guarded secret."

"Sounds great." Tony turned his sparkling black eyes toward Cole in anticipation. It was at that exact moment that Cole truly lost his heart to his son.

Eight

"**O**f course I remember you, Allison," Cameron said, standing in the hallway on his crutches, grinning. He'd had the walking cast for a couple of weeks. The cast had come off his arm the week before. "I had the biggest crush on you when I was growing up. You were my idea of the perfect woman."

Cole and Tony had their bags still in their arms when Allison had opened the door and held it for them. What he didn't need at the moment was for his brother to be gushing over their houseguest. He glanced at Allison. She had a delightful confusion about her, which gave her an even more attractive glow. She didn't need to look any more attractive than she already did.

"Why, thank you, Cam," she managed to say with a husky laugh.

Cameron sighed. "There's just something about you older women that can really get to a guy." He pretended to dodge her expected retaliation and turned to Tony. "Hi! You must be Tony. I'm Cameron, Cole's brother. His much younger brother."

"All right, all right. You made your point." Cole turned to the others. "He's really become incorrigible since he's been home. Too much free time. I can hardly wait to ship him back to the office."

Tony turned and looked at Cameron. "I'm very pleased to meet you, sir."

"Ah, now here's someone who knows how to show some respect."

Cole drawled, "Oh, Cameron, why don't you have Tony share with you his views on real estate versus oil investments over the profit margins of raising cattle?" Cole's smile couldn't be more innocent. "Meanwhile I'll show Allison where they'll be staying." He motioned to Allison to follow him up the stairs, wishing he'd had a camera to capture the look on Cam's face when Tony accepted the choice of subject and started to talk.

Cole chuckled to himself all the way up the stairs.

"Cameron seems to be adjusting well to everything that happened, hasn't he?"

"Don't kid yourself. He's keeping it all bottled up inside. One of these days he's going to blow."

"Oh. I remember him as very quiet. Really shy."

Cole gave her a wolfish grin. "I'm sure he was, around you."

She shook her head in a gesture signifying the futility of having a serious conversation at the moment.

He stopped in front of one of the doors, put the luggage down, then opened the door. "I thought I'd put you in here. It will be a little more convenient for you, as this room has a bathroom attached." He set her bag just inside the door, then continued down the hallway. "I

thought I'd put Tony in here. This was Cody's old room.
Rather than take down all the posters and things, he just
moved to a bigger bedroom." He turned to her. "Do you
realize that Tony is the same age difference with Cody as
I am with Cody? They could easily be brothers."

"Except they aren't."

He didn't look at her, but set the suitcase at the end of
the bed. When he turned to look at her, he could see the
pain in her eyes. Forgetting his own apprehension, Cole
walked over to Allison and slipped his arms around her
waist. "It's going to work out all right. You'll see. I'm
just glad to have you both here."

She slipped her arms around his waist, hanging on to
his belt loops in the back. "All of this seems so strange."

He leaned back so that he could see her face. "How do
you mean?"

"I don't feel that I should be upstairs. In all the years
I lived on the ranch, I was never upstairs. I could visit in
certain designated rooms downstairs, but not up here. I
don't feel like I belong here."

"Oh, honey, that isn't true. Who told you that you
couldn't come up here?"

"It was never said out loud. It was just something that
I understood from a very early age."

"Then it's time to get rid of those ideas, okay? Come
on. Let's show Tony around the place. I'd like you to see
some of the changes we've made, as well."

By the time Allison retired to her room that night, her
head ached with confusion and anxiety. She felt as
though she were in some kind of a time warp, as though
the past fifteen years had never happened, as though
she'd never left the ranch, her father had never died,
everything had continued on. And then she would glance

around and see Tony eagerly asking questions... touching, patting, stroking, looking at everything around him, absorbing it all like a tall, gangly sponge.

She ached for him. All of this should have been a part of his growing up. How could she possibly let him know the truth? How could she explain all of the circumstances? He'd never heard of Letitia Callaway, and she sincerely hoped he never did.

Even now, standing in the spacious bedroom that Cole had given to her, she felt guilty—as though Letty might burst in at any moment and tell her to get out!

What a bunch of nonsense. She was just tired, that's all. She hadn't been able to sleep last night except for short intervals. All she could think about was the fact that she was returning to the past she'd tried so hard to forget. As soon as they had turned off the highway onto the ranch road, she had known that this homecoming was going to be even more painful than she could have guessed.

She had immediately spotted the changes that had updated and modernized the place. The new Spanish tile roof sparkled in the sunlight, a brilliant contrast to the dazzling-white freshly painted adobe.

This time they didn't take the lane down to the married quarters, but pulled up in front of the ten-foot-high door. She was a guest, now—a guest of the Callaways.

Looking around the bedroom, she reminded herself of that fact. Well, then, she would enjoy her new status to the fullest.

She walked over to the door of the bathroom and peered inside. This one displayed all the latest innovations a luxurious bathroom could possibly have. A square Jacuzzi tub took up almost one whole wall. There were steps leading up to it. A double-size shower stall with glass panels on three sides was on another wall. The long countertop had two sinks. The mirrors reflected each other—one above the counter, the other an entire wall of mirrors.

She'd never seen anything quite so decadent or more inviting. With a giggle she hadn't heard out of herself since she was a child, Allison began to run her bathwater.

The shelves along the side of the tub had an array of bath oils, soaps and other toiletries. She hurried back into the bedroom only to discover that someone had been in earlier and unpacked her things. She found her sleep shirt in the second drawer she opened.

By the time she returned, the tub was full. She noted a large pillar candle on the shelf with a small package of matches. On impulse, she lighted the candle, then turned out the overhead light. Immediately the mirrors caught and reflected the soft glow of the candlelight, softening the edges of her world. She slipped out of her clothes and stepped into the tub.

The water felt heavenly to her tired body. She touched a switch that started the jets on all sides of her. Slowly she dropped her head back on the padded side of the tub and closed her eyes. She felt like the pampered darling of the rich and famous.

The slight click she heard sounded like a door opening, which couldn't be possible, she thought, opening her eyes. They continued to widen. Cole walked into the bathroom from a door on the opposite side of the one she'd entered from. He wore a short, bright green terry robe.

The water's continual churning had created a concealing froth of foam; nevertheless Allison sank into the water up to her chin.

"What are you doing here?" she tried to say, but ended up choking on some bubbles that popped into her mouth as soon as she opened it, so that the end of the sentence came out in a sputter. He seemed to understand her well enough, however.

He raised his brows. "Oh, didn't I tell you?" he asked in an innocent voice. "Our rooms share the same bath."

"No," she managed to say in a strangled tone, "you neglected to mention that *insignificant* little fact."

"Oh." He glanced around the room, then back at her. "This is my favorite part of the day, when I can come in here after a hard day and relax. I see you found the candle. The light's much better like that, isn't it?"

He reached for the sash of his robe.

"What do you think you're doing?"

He looked a little puzzled. "You don't mind if I share the tub with you, do you? I mean, there's plenty of room for two without crowding."

While she was trying to spit out her objection, *Yes, I certainly do mind,* the words soon lost their purpose because he'd discarded his robe and stepped into the tub.

The sight of his massive, nude body took her breath away, effectively demolishing her communicating abilities.

She hadn't seen a grown man nude before, she realized now. The changes that she had only guessed at when she saw Cole again were now vividly and advantageously displayed. His broad chest was liberally covered with hair. His arms and shoulders were immense. His hips and thighs were—she closed her eyes with fierce determination while she felt the turbulent action of the water shift to accommodate his bulk.

He'd been right. There was room for two, as long as they didn't mind their legs intertwining. With a nonchalance that she could only marvel at, Cole lightly lifted her ankles and placed them on each side of his hips. His calves, ankles and feet were meanwhile insidiously enfolding her thighs and hips.

She heard his sigh of pleasure. "Isn't this great? I just had this bathroom redone last winter, but it was well worth the inconvenience and expense. Guaranteed to make all those aches and pains go away."

He didn't mention the aches that it suddenly created.

"Cole, you have no business coming in here and you know it. How do you think Tony would react if he knew you were in here with me?"

"Is there any reason for him to find out?"

"Of course not, it's just—"

"It's no one's business what you do in the privacy of your own bathroom, is it?"

"The point is—"

"The point is that you're supposed to be relaxing and now you're getting all tensed up." He ran his hands along her legs, from thighs to calves, kneading the muscles.

"Cole! Stop that!"

"Relax, honey. I'm not going to take advantage of you."

"What do you think you've just done? You placed me in a room where you knew we would be sharing a bath, but you didn't bother to tell me. You wait until I'm in a very vulnerable position, then walk in on me. You..." She seemed to run out of words.

"Yes?" he asked helpfully, lifting a brow.

"Would you please get out until I'm through with my bath?"

"No. Anything else?" he asked with a smile.

"Fine. Then I'll get out and you can have your bath and your fancy—" She had been matching actions with words until it suddenly occurred to her that if she were to crawl out of the tub at this particular moment, she would be even more exposed.

Allison slid back into the water up to her chin and glared at him.

"Come on, relax and enjoy yourself, honey. I promise I won't bite." His grin suddenly flashed. "Of course I might consider doing a little nibblin' here and there, if I was coaxed." Cole picked up the hand soap and began to smooth it across his broad and brawny chest.

Determined to ignore his provocative comment, Allison focused on his movements and slowly found herself mesmerized by his sensual actions. The thick hair on his chest swirled as the soap and water coaxed them into patterns.

Once again she became aware of how good the water felt swirling around her. There was no reason for her to get into such an uproar. She was certainly in no danger.

Aren't you? a nagging little voice asked. When was the last time you reacted to a man like you're reacting now?

How was she supposed to act, for heaven's sake? She'd never been in a bath with a man before.

"Cole, why are you doing this?"

His eyes met hers. "All I've been able to think about for the past several weeks was this visit. I went over and over what it would be like to have you back here on the ranch. What it came down to was that I wanted to get close to you again. I wanted to reestablish the line of communication we had all our lives. I know we can't just forget about what happened or dismiss the past fifteen years, but I want to overcome the pain we both went through.'' He shrugged. ''I don't want the visit to be a polite gesture. We scarcely talked today because of the people around us. I need more than that. I think we both do.'' He spread his soapy hands, ''So, here we are, getting reacquainted.''

''I won't make love to you,'' she stated firmly.

''Thanks for the information, honey, but I haven't asked.''

She could feel her face heating up. ''Just so we understand each other,'' she muttered.

''Now that we have that out of the way, come here and let me scrub your back.'' Saying that he reached for her and pulled her toward him, turning her as she came closer so that her back was to him.

He began to knead the muscles at the back of her skull, whispering in a low voice, ''Relax,'' as he continued to work down each vertebra of her spine. The combination of knowledgeable touch and soothing tone soon took effect and she began to relax against him. Eventually she realized he was no longer stroking her back. Now she lay against his chest while his arms encircled her waist.

In this position she had no trouble recognizing that he was aroused. His hands lightly stroked her midriff, occasionally brushing the underside of her breasts, which felt full and tingling.

Allison knew that she should be protesting the intimacy of the situation, but a sense of lethargy had taken over . . . her limbs felt heavy, as did her eyelids. Her neck no longer felt strong enough to support her head, and she allowed it to droop against Cole's shoulder. She closed her eyes and sighed in contentment.

''Allison?''

"Hmm."

"I want you to think about something for me during the next couple of weeks, and give me your answer then, not now."

"What is it?" she murmured drowsily.

"I want you to marry me so that you and Tony and I can be together all the time, not just a few days here and there."

An alarm began jangling within her head. She began to stir.

"No, don't start trying to find something negative to say about that statement. I just want you to think about what I've said. I wanted you to know what I want, what I'm planning to work for. You don't have to remind me that I wasn't there when you needed me. I know that. What I'm saying to you is that I want to be there now and for the rest of our lives, not just because you might need me, but because I know in the very depths of my being how very much I need you to make my life whole. I've spent the past fifteen years without you and I've managed. I'd prefer not to continue my life without you." He nudged her head aside slightly and placed a row of fleeting kisses along the side of her neck. "So you think about it, honey, all right? We'll talk about it before you leave."

He eased away from her, then stood, water cascading off him so that she held up her hands in a protective gesture and gasped. He stepped out of the tub and walked down the steps. After toweling himself briskly he pulled the terry robe around him. "Don't drown in there now, you hear?" His smile was wistful as he silently closed the door behind him, leaving her to the solitude of flickering candlelight and the soft sounds of bubbling water.

Allison blinked her eyes a couple of times in an effort to make sure she was awake. She hadn't dreamed the past half hour, had she? Cole had actually walked in on her, hadn't he?

And done what? Caused her to become more aware of him than she had thought possible. She'd known as soon as she made the decision to come to the ranch that she would have to guard herself against his charismatic presence, but she had thought herself safe in the haven of her room and bath.

So what should she do now? Demand another room? Keep the door locked when she was in there? Or wait to see what developed in the coming weeks?

She smiled to herself.

What would be wrong with enjoying her time on the ranch, facing and releasing old memories and hurts, and collecting new, more joyful memories to take back home with her?

She reluctantly pushed the button that stopped the jets, and the water slowly swirled to a few ripples as she got out, feeling a complete lassitude that was belied by the inner excitement that raced through every atom of her being.

The feel of the towel against her sensitive skin made her excruciatingly aware of her body as it brushed across her shoulders and down her back, over her buttocks and the back of her thighs, knees and calves. She returned her attention to her throat and down across her breasts and their rigid tips, down her stomach and abdomen, the gentle brush of cloth causing a tingling that made her shiver with—

"I almost forgot," a low voice said behind her. She looked into the mirror and saw Cole's reflection standing in the doorway as though he'd been watching her for some time. Allison's heart bounded in her chest, more from excitement than fear. Her back was bare, as was her upper torso. Their eyes met in the mirror and he slowly advanced, sliding his arms around her and palming her breasts. "Allison, you are so beautiful." He kissed her on the nape of her neck, his hair brushing against her jaw. As though she were no more than a windup mechanical toy, Allison slowly turned in his arms until she was facing him, her neck arched so that her lips were only a hairbreadth away from his. She came up on her toes until her mouth pressed against his, feeling their firmness gentle and warm at her touch. Audaciously she flicked her tongue across them. He made a growling sound in the back of his throat and scooped her up into his arms without lessening the pressure of his mouth.

Allison's head spun from the sudden movement. The only solid, dependable point in her universe at the moment was Cole, and she clung to him, her arms around his neck, her mouth yielding to his.

The next sensations she became aware of were the softness of finely woven sheets at her back and his weight on top of her. When he raised his head for a moment they both took in great gasps of air before he sought her breast with his tongue, stroking, flicking and rolling the pink tip in energetic play. She arched her back, holding his head against her.

He ran his callused palms along her sides and down her thighs, smoothing, then inciting a response. Each stroke brought his hands closer to her inner thighs until he paused at the top of her inner thigh and touched her inquiringly.

Any doubt as to her readiness for him was immediately dispelled. She undulated her hips, moving as close to him as she could with his weight pinning her down. He shifted, so that she could ease her legs wider apart, giving her the freedom she needed to arch up into him.

This time his groan was mixed with a muttering of, "I'm sorry, honey, but I can't—" before he plunged deeply inside.

Allison no longer cared what it was he couldn't. She was all too aware of just what he could—and was—doing to give her pleasure.

The years had faded her memories of the only other time this man had made love to her. There was no comparison she could make at the moment. All she could do was to feel and respond to his touch and masculine scent, to the sound of his harsh breathing and the taste of him on her lips.

The fast fury of their coming together was too intense to be prolonged. She felt herself suddenly contract, then begin a series of spasmodic movements deep inside that caused him to lose what little remaining control he had.

He cried out as he made a convulsive movement, burying himself deep within her. He wrapped his arms around her and held her tightly, almost sobbing with the intensity of the moment.

A longing never to let go of him swept over her, and she squeezed him to her, her legs wrapped fiercely around his thighs. He sighed and rolled so that they lay side by side, locked into each other's arms, his eyes closed. His face was flushed and damp. She smiled, touching her finger to his cheek. He opened his eyes and stared into hers a short distance away.

"That wasn't part of the plan," he murmured ruefully.

"Oh?"

"No. What I intended to do was to make you aware of me on a more physical basis."

"You certainly managed to do that."

"What I mean is, I wanted you to want me. I hoped to get past that barrier you've had around you ever since my first visit to Mason."

"Well, you succeeded there."

"I thought I would have more self-control. I thought I could see you and touch you without taking it any further."

"Ah. You planned to get me all stirred up and then walk away?"

He gave her a tentative, half smile. "Something like that."

"How ungentlemanly of you."

"Perhaps."

"Tonight doesn't prove anything, Cole."

"It proves that we're both very compatible in bed."

"But it isn't a reason to base a decision on."

"It's a hell of a start."

"Cole, we were a couple of kids before who knew nothing about what we wanted in life."

"Speak for yourself. I always knew what I wanted. Nothing's changed."

"*I've* changed, Cole. I'm no longer the little pigtailed girl that used to follow you everywhere."

He ran his hand down her side, tracing her curves. "I'll admit to some changes, but I see nothing wrong with them."

"I've been on my own for a long time, Cole. I've learned to appreciate my freedom and my independence."

"Do you think that I'm asking you to give those up?"

"Aren't you?"

"Hell, no. I'm proud as punch you've made a name for yourself, that you found your talents and developed them. All I'm saying is that I want you in my life."

"You want me . . . or Tony?"

He leaned up on his elbow and stared down at her. "What are you saying?"

She stared at him for several moments before she admitted, "I'm not certain. All I know is that I've never made any effort to hide from you in all these years, yet you showed no interest in looking me up...until you met Tony. I can understand your desire to get to know your son, Cole. Just don't think that you have to include me in your plans. It doesn't have to be a package deal."

His eyes narrowed and he pulled away from her. Rolling over he flipped on the bedside lamp and reached for his cigarettes. He took his time lighting one, drawing in the smoke for a long moment before exhaling. Finally he glanced around at her. "I don't think this is a good time to discuss Tony, or you, for that matter. If you can think that I would make love to you the way I did just now as part of a plot to have Tony in my life, then you're right, I don't know you very well. And just as important, you sure as hell don't know me."

The tender lover was gone. For a brief moment Allison felt a wave of despair wash over her as a memory of her grief years before resurfaced. Why had she thought that they could talk about all that had happened without touching some nerves that were still raw?

She reached for his crumpled bathrobe and slipped it around her, then left the bed. "You see, Cole? Sex never solved a thing." She turned away from him and started to the door.

"Is that what it was for you, Allison? A little romp in the hay? No wonder you've stayed single all these years, if it's just a temporary moment of pleasure to you. Afterward you can forget it and walk away."

She paused, then turned and looked at him as he sat there on the side of the bed, nude, smoking his cigarette.

"Don't start throwing accusations at me, Cole. I haven't heard about you running to the altar in the past fifteen years."

"You're damn right. I learned at an early age that women can't be trusted to mean what they say."

Her smile was wry. "Funny, but I learned the same lesson about men. I guess we're more alike than I first thought. Good night, Cole."

She turned and walked out of the room, leaving him to stare at the closed door that symbolized all that stood between them.

Nine

"How can you stand to live anywhere else, Cole?" Tony asked the next day while they were out riding.

Cole had spent a sleepless night wrestling with ghosts of the past. The early-morning ride he'd planned had been his reason for going back into the bathroom the night before. He'd waited until morning to tap on Allison's bedroom door and ask if she wanted to go with him and Tony.

When she'd joined them downstairs at the breakfast table she didn't look as though she had slept any better than he had. Dark circles lay beneath her heavy-lidded eyes. Although they had been out riding for some time now, she had yet to say a word to either of them, seemingly content to ride over old haunts and renew her memories of the place.

Tony was doing what he could to keep the conversation going.

"It's difficult, I'll admit," Cole finally said. "But I have other businesses to run besides the ranch. That's why I leave the running of this place to the others."

"Like Cameron and Cody?"

"Well, Cameron works fairly closely with me. And Cody, well, I'm not sure that Cody's decided what he wants to do when he settles down. He's in and out of here, but pretty much goes his own way."

"Then who looks after the place?"

"We have a main foreman, and several others who take care of specific areas, and of course my aunt—" Oh, hell, now he'd done it.

"Your aunt?"

"Uh, yeah. She usually oversees the running of the Big House and the domestic duties . . . that kind of thing."

"How come I haven't seen her?"

"Oh, she's away right now," he said, looking off into the hills to avoid both Allison and Tony.

"Will she be back before we have to leave?"

"I don't think so."

"Oh."

Letty was another problem he'd have to deal with if he was to convince Allison to take a chance on him again. Damn, but he was tired of juggling all of the pieces of his life so that everyone was treated fairly. No matter what she had done, Letty was family. She'd held the family together for years after his folks had died. Somehow, someway, he needed to bring things together in such a way that Allison would accept all of his family as well as him.

After last night, he felt that his battle was definitely uphill. She was probably more apt to accept Letty at the moment than she was him. He'd let his foolish emotions overwhelm him the night before. It was such a stupid mistake to lose control like that. He must have thought he was above succumbing to temptation. Well, he'd sure as hell learned differently.

"Cole?"

Tony's voice broke through Cole's preoccupation with his thoughts, and he realized that Tony had repeated his name a couple of times with no response.

"Sorry, I guess my mind drifted away for a moment," he said with a smile to the teenager riding alongside of him.

"No problem. Mom does that a lot, too," he explained with a grin. "So I'm used to it. I was just wondering where your property lines are. It seems like we've ridden for a few hours and haven't seen anything but occasional cattle and windmills pumping water in reservoirs."

Cole paused and looked around. They had come a fair distance from the ranch buildings. Once he got his bearings, he pointed to a line of rolling hills in the distance. "Those hills mark the northern boundary. The western boundary is near the Mexican border at the Rio Grande."

Tony's eyes widened. "But that's miles and miles."

"That's right."

"Wow!" He glanced around at his mother. "Did you know the Circle C was that big, Mom? It's as big as the King Ranch in south Texas."

"Not quite," Cole admitted, "but close."

Allison wore dark sunshades today as well as a Stetson pulled low over her forehead, so that her eyes were completely hidden and her face was in shadows. "I hate to call a halt to all this fun, fellas," she finally said in a rueful voice, "but it's been awhile since I've been on a horse. If we don't turn back soon, I'll be sitting on a pillow for the next few days."

Tony laughed and glanced at Cole. "Guess we should have left her at home, huh?"

Not on your life, Cole thought to himself. Not with Cameron waiting to entertain her. His thoughts moved to Cody. And where was his younger brother? Surely he'd found out something about the accidents by now.

"Actually, I do need to get back soon. I've got a conference call coming in at eleven."

Even while he spoke, Cole felt a helpless sense of frustration. There was so much he wanted to say to Allison that couldn't be said in front of Tony, and so much he wanted to say to Tony but couldn't. At least, not until he could tell him the truth. He felt as though he'd had his ankles and wrists tied and was expected to function normally.

For the first time in a long while he was faced with a situation over which he had no control. He didn't like it. Hell, he wasn't used to it. He glanced over at Allison who had yet to look at him directly since she'd come downstairs that morning.

What more could he say? He'd been a class-A jerk the night before. What good would an apology do now?

By the time he got off the conference call it was almost one o'clock. When he went looking for the others he found Tony and Cameron in a hot game of poker.

"Where's your mother?" he asked with what he hoped was a casual tone.

Tony glanced around. "Oh, she went upstairs after lunch. Said she was already getting sore from the ride." He flashed the grin that reminded Cole of his Callaway blood. "Guess she's having a tough time keeping up with us, huh?"

Cameron was stretched out on his side on the couch, playing cards off the coffee table, while Tony sat cross-legged on the floor. Cameron glanced up at Cole. "You look a little weary, old man. Why don't you get yourself a nap? I'll entertain the young 'un here."

Rosie came in, carrying a tray of lemonade and cookies. "Did you save me any lunch?" Cole asked.

"Of course. Do you want me to bring it to you?"

"No. Just tell me where it is."

"It's on a covered tray in the refrigerator."

He went looking for it, pausing to glance into the garden room. Originally part of the interior patio, they had glassed a portion of the area in so that it could be air-conditioned. Trisha lay sound asleep in her playpen, her stuffed animals all around her.

Cole had such a yearning for a daughter just like her, one that he and Allison could raise together, one that—

A sudden thought struck him, one that should have surfaced long before now. Oh, no. Oh, hell! He strode into the kitchen and opened the refrigerator. A salad and several sandwiches awaited him. He ate them at the breakfast bar, perched on the edge of the stool, needing to eat but regretting the time it took. He needed to talk with Allison. He needed to find out if— What an unthinking idiot he was. He'd never once thought . . .

He placed his dishes in the sink, finished off his second glass of milk and bounded up the stairs. Allison's door was closed. She could be asleep. If so, he wouldn't waken her. He went into his bedroom and began to strip out of his clothes. He needed a shower after that long ride this morning. He stepped into their shared bathroom and instantly caught the scent of her perfume. Her brush and comb lay on the shelf above one of the sinks. He smiled, enjoying the sight of their things sharing the same space.

After finishing his shower, he dried off and went back into his room to dress. He was just about finished buttoning his shirt when he thought he heard a noise from the other room. Still barefoot, he padded into the connecting room and pushed slightly against her door. It swung open noiselessly, revealing Allison in her robe lying on the bed on her stomach, her eyes closed, a frown etched across her forehead.

"What's wrong?" he whispered, in case she was still asleep.

She opened her eyes and saw him. "Don't you ever knock?" she demanded without moving.

"I didn't want to wake you in case you were asleep."

"I hurt too much to sleep."

"Why didn't you say something earlier?"

"And spoil the fun? I haven't seen Tony that animated since his favorite country-western singer appeared in concert in Austin."

"Hold on." He went back into the bathroom and opened the medicine cabinet. Grabbing a bottle, he returned to Allison's room, strode across to the bed and sank onto the side.

"What are you doing?"

"I'm going to give you some relief," he said with a grin.

"I just bet you are!"

"No, I mean it," he reassured her. He began to slide her satin robe up her legs. She pushed up on her elbows with a groan and said, "Cole, you are taking unfair advantage of a crippled person. Now please go away."

He began to laugh. "Honey, I promise that what I intend to do will only give you pleasure, not to mention easing the pain." By the time he'd finished his reassuring speech he'd slid the material to her waist, exposing a delectable backside that he determinedly refused to admire. Detachment was the key.

He warmed the liniment in the palms of his hands, then gently laid his palms on each bared cheek. She flinched. "There now, honey, you're okay," he said in a soothing tone.

"Don't talk to me like—ouch—I'm some kind of—oohh—filly you're trying to calm."

"Wouldn't think of it," he agreed, hiding his grin by looking away.

He ran his hands down the back of her thighs to her knees, then slowly moved them upward, rubbing in a circular motion, until he reached her buttocks once more. He continued the movements until he felt her muscles beginning to relax beneath his experienced fingers. He moved along her legs, sliding his thumbs to her inner thighs and moving them in a circular motion, moving upward by infinitesimal degrees.

Her sighs and moans became more muted and less based on pain. By the time he paused at the top of her inner thighs she was breathing softly and regularly, her eyes closed.

Silently he moved off the bed, capped the liniment bottle and returned to the bathroom. After putting away the medication, he looked ruefully at the shower and contemplated the soothing relief of cold water hitting his overheated body.

Stoically he reminded himself that he'd just showered and he could get his thoughts on other things. He returned to his bedroom and finished dressing, then headed down the stairs. By the time he reached the bottom he could hear Cameron and Tony talking.

"What I don't understand," Tony was saying, "was how come Mom never told me that she knew you guys? I mean, the Callaways are famous. There's always some news about one of you doing something, or winning something or buying something. She sat and watched all of that without saying a word. Don't you find that strange?''

Cole waited to see what Cameron replied, glad that for once *he* wasn't the recipient of Tony's pointed questions.

''Guess you'll have to ask your mom about that. Nobody knows what's going on in another person's head, Tony. It's sheer arrogance to think we can guess.''

''Well, I'm beginning to think there's something fishy going on.''

''What do you mean?''

''I think Mom and Cole had a fight . . . like maybe a lovers' quarrel or something.''

Cole realized that he was standing just outside the study blatantly eavesdropping. He also recognized that he wasn't about to let his presence be known at this point. He waited for Cameron to respond.

''What makes you think that?''

''It's the way they look at each other, you know? The way they look when they don't think the other is looking. A guy could get scorched if he got caught in the middle of one of those looks.'' Cameron started laughing and Tony reluctantly chuckled. ''It's kinda weird, thinking about my mom interested in somebody.''

''I thought you said she was seeing someone.''

''Oh, yeah, but that's different. I mean, Ed happens to be in town once or twice a month. They're more friends than anything. Mom doesn't tense up or get all flustered and bothered around Ed like she does Cole.''

''Is that right? Interesting.''

''Do you think they had a fight?''

"If they did, no one ever mentioned it to me. Of course, I was your age when your mom and grandfather moved away."

"Did you know my dad?"

A pregnant pause followed that one and Cole smiled to himself, wondering if it wasn't time to rescue Cameron.

"Don't believe I did."

"See? That's another thing. How come nobody remembers him? It seems to me—"

"So who's winning?" Cole asked, strolling into the room with his hands in his pockets. Cameron looked at him like a drowning man suddenly tossed a life preserver.

Tony glanced around. "Cameron is."

The three men looked down at the poker chips scattered across the table.

"You can take my place," Cameron said, reaching for his crutches. "I think I'm going to take a nap. It's been a busy day." He glanced at Tony, then gave Cole a meaningful look.

Cole sat on the couch after Cameron left. "Did Cameron tell you why he's on crutches?"

"Yeah, he mentioned it. That's too bad, losing his wife and all."

"Have you seen his daughter?"

Tony's face lit up. "Oh, yeah, Rosie brought her in awhile ago after her nap. She's a real cutie."

"I think so."

"Cole, how come you never married? I mean, here you are the head of the family and all, don't you want to have children to leave all of this to someday?"

Why couldn't this kid talk about cars and girls and the latest rock group like every other teenager Cole had met?

"Have you ever thought about a career in journalism?" Cole asked, reaching for a cigarette.

Tony looked puzzled. "No, why?"

"Because you have a hell of an interviewing technique."

"Does that mean I'm being too nosy?"

"Well, I have to admit I never know what's going to come out of your mouth."

"But how do you learn about things unless you ask?"

"There is that, of course. Well, as to any marriage plans I might have, I—"

The front door slammed and the rapid tattoo of boot heels on the tiled floor in the hallway preceded a voice, calling, "Where is everybody?"

Cole grinned and winked at Tony. "In here, Cody." Then he came to his feet. Cody rounded the corner and came to an abrupt halt when he saw Tony getting up from his position on the floor. He stared at first one, then the other, his face a marvel of mixed expressions.

"Come on in, Cody, and meet Tony Alvarez. Tony, this is my youngest brother, Cody."

Tony held out his hand awkwardly. "Pleased to meet you, Cody," he said diffidently.

Cody took in the boy standing there before him, his eyes widening at the Callaway likeness. Then he took his hand and shook it. "Glad to meet you, Tony. Didn't know you were going to be visiting us."

"Uh, yeah. Me and my mom arrived yesterday."

"Allison's here?" he asked, looking at Cole in surprise.

"I would have told you if you'd ever bother checking in once in a while."

Cody grinned at his brother's peeved tone. "Sorry. I'm not used to having to report to someone."

Cole raised his brow. "Letty didn't have as much influence over you as I would have guessed."

Cody laughed. "You got that right. She considers me incorrigible. So!" He glanced back at Tony. "How long are you staying?"

"A couple of weeks."

"Great. We'll have to get together and do something, get acquainted."

"How did you know my mom was Allison Alvarez?"

"Because only Allison would have named her son Tony Alvarez," he replied immediately.

Cole knew that Tony wasn't going to be put off by half answers for long. He needed to talk to Allison about the situation and soon.

He waited until after she left the bathroom that night before tapping on her door. He even waited until she said "Come in," before opening it. He found her at the vanity brushing out her hair.

"We need to talk."

"Go ahead," she said noncommittally.

"About Tony."

She stopped running the brush through her hair and stared at him in the mirror. "What about Tony?"

Cole began to pace. "Look. This is one brilliant kid we've got here. He's quick to put things together and he's already asking questions. I don't want to lie to him."

"What sort of questions?"

"About his father, for one thing. Remember he was asking me, then today I overheard him questioning Cameron." He turned and looked at Allison. "He's got to be told the truth, Allison."

She looked down at her hands. "Is this the first step in turning him into a Callaway?"

He moved over to where she sat and knelt beside her. "Honey, you know better than that. Whether you want to hear it or not, I love you. I have always loved you. I will always love you. I told you last night that I want to marry you. I mean that. Can't you see that we need to sit with Tony—together—and explain to him what happened?"

"Putting the blame on my father and your aunt?"

"Forget blaming. Just tell him the truth. We made a mistake, okay? We're human. Tony is going to have to accept that." He slid his arms around her waist and hugged her to him, his head resting on her breast.

Slowly she ran her fingers through his hair, loving the silkiness of it, reminded of the number of times she'd held Tony in her lap and done the same thing. She loved both of them so much. She felt torn between wanting to protect her son from hurt and wanting him to understand his heritage.

"You're right, of course," she finally said, sighing. "I can't continue to protect him indefinitely from the truth, particularly now that he's met you."

"Will you let me tell him that we're going to get married?"

"No!" She straightened, dropping her arms. "It's too soon to consider."

"Not necessarily. Unless you're on some form of birth control, we could easily have begun another child last night, or haven't you thought about that?"

She stared at him in horror.

"From that look I would say that there's a distinct possibility," he said, when she didn't say anything.

"Oh, Cole," she finally whispered. "I never thought about it. Not once. I can't believe I was so irresponsible... after what I went through with Tony."

"Neither one of us was thinking very clearly last night, and that was my fault, I'm afraid."

Tears began to roll down her cheeks. "I never wanted you to marry me because you *had* to."

"Honey, I would never feel that I had to, can't you understand that? What do I have to say to convince you I love you?"

She wiped her hands across her eyes, not answering.

Cole felt the familiar gnawing of frustration at not being able to control the outcome. "Why don't we talk to him tomorrow? We'll take a picnic lunch out near one of the creeks."

"No more riding for me for a few days," Allison warned him.

"We can go in one of the trucks. We'll get away, just the three of us, and I'll explain. What do you think?"

"At this point, we don't have much of a choice."

He rose, then took her hand and lifted her from the vanity seat, slowly drawing her into his arms. "He's your son, darlin'...filled with courage and full of compassion. He'll understand, I'm sure of it."

She tried to smile, but it wobbled on her lips. "He's also your son, impetuous and hot-tempered. He's not going to like knowing he's been lied to, Cole. Don't ever think he will."

"Granted. But he'll listen to our explanations, won't he?"

"I hope so. I can only hope he'll linger long enough to listen to what we have to say before he bolts."

Ten

"**Y**ou're making this up, right?" Tony said, staring at Allison and Cole.

They had just finished off the contents of a large picnic basket and were resting in the shade of a cottonwood tree near a small creek not too far from the Big House.

Before Cole could respond, Tony added hoarsely, "It's because you don't want me to know about my real father." He turned to Allison, his eyes filled with pain. "You've always been afraid of telling me about him, haven't you? He was somebody bad, someone you were ashamed of. So you and Cole have decided to make up some lie to tell me."

Her eyes met Cole's for a moment before she looked at Tony. "I've never been ashamed of your father, Tony. Your grandfather was the one who made up the story about my brief marriage. Whether it was the wrong thing or the right thing to do, I never corrected it, even after he died. I suppose I found the established situation easier to go along with as you grew up. I could see no reason to drag up the past because I thought it was all behind me. I never expected to see or hear from Cole again, so it didn't seem to matter who your father was.''

Tony stared at her in despair. ''Not matter! How could it not matter? All these years I thought my father was dead, that I had no one but you. And now…'' He looked at Cole, his eyes accusing. ''If you're really my father, how come I'm just hearing about it *now?*''

''Because I never knew you existed until that day we met on the beach, Tony. Believe me, I would never have allowed you or your mother out of my life if I had known about you.''

Tony's accusing gaze met Allison's. ''Why didn't he know? Why didn't you tell him about me? Why did you have to keep me a secret?''

She took a deep breath and said, ''I thought he did know, Tony. It's only been since we've seen each other again that I discovered he never received any of the letters I wrote, so of course he didn't know about my pregnancy. All he knew was that we'd moved away suddenly. He didn't know where we were or how to contact me. It was a series of happenings that neither of us could have anticipated.''

''You're always harping about my being responsible and how everyone needs to practice safe sex and all, and here you're telling me that you and—'' He paused and gulped. ''I don't believe this. It's just too weird. I mean, I run into some guy on the beach and now you're telling me that—'' He shook his head in bewilderment, then sprang to his feet. ''You've been lying to me my whole life! You've pretended that my dad died when all the time he was somebody I could have gotten to know. You lied to me!''

He spun away and raced up the incline and over the hill toward the road back to the Big House.

Allison sprang to her feet. ''Tony! Wait! We—''

''Let him go,'' Cole said in a low voice behind her. ''Give him a chance to get used to the idea. It's all so new to him.''

''He's going to hate me,'' she said in a choked voice.

''Why do you say that?''

''Because I lied to him about you. He's going to remember how much I talked about the need to be honest and to tell the truth, regardless of how much he might get into trouble.'' She moved her hands restlessly. ''Now he'll see how I didn't follow my own beliefs.''

She hurt inside, so much so that she felt as though she were in a vise that continued to squeeze her harder and harder. ''I didn't want him hurt. He's so young! I wanted him to see that I love him, and that I was only trying to protect him.''

Cole stood and pulled her into his arms. ''He knows you love him, Allison. I promise you, he knows. But he has to work through this on his own, don't you understand? It's time to stop trying to protect him. He deserves to know the truth and to act on it in any way he chooses. What we have to do is to give him the space to feel all of those conflicting emotions that are tearing through him at the moment. He's got to be able to cry if he feels like it, curse if it helps, scream and shout.'' He glanced around them. ''This is where he can do that, don't you see?''

She, too, glanced around. ''But what if he gets lost?''

''He won't—we're too close to the house. But what he needs is time to get some perspective on all of this. Remember when he told me in the car that it wasn't as important to him where he came from as much as where he was going?''

She nodded, wiping the silent tears streaming down her cheeks. Cole continued in a gentle voice. "Now is his chance to see how deeply he carries his belief. He is still the same person. Nothing has really changed except how he sees himself. He needs time to adjust, but he'll do it. I know he will."

She pulled away and knelt, placing the picnic remains in the basket. "He feels so betrayed."

"Yes. He *was* betrayed. So were you. So was I. From a more mature perspective I can see where we might have done things differently. You could have telephoned me when I didn't answer your first letters...I could have insisted on finding out where the two of you had moved. But what each of us needs to see is that at that time in our lives we were doing the very best we could. Regrets over past actions are the most futile waste of energy there is. What I hoped to do today was to give Tony the heritage that he didn't know he had. It was as painful for me to tell him as it was for you to listen to and for him to hear. But it had to be done."

He picked up the blanket and repacked basket and placed them in the truck. "Give him some time, okay? I have a hunch he'll come around eventually. At least he now knows the truth."

As they drove back to the Big House, Allison spoke in a low voice. "I thought I'd come to terms with my past," she said slowly, "until we arrived here. Being here again has brought back so many memories."

"Not all bad, I hope."

"No, but painful, nonetheless. I emotionally buried the young girl who lived here...and now, all at once, she's alive and feeling everything all over again.'' She turned her head so that she was looking at Cole's profile. "I'm not at all certain I want this much feeling in my life. I was content before. I had Tony and my work. I had peace of mind. All of that is so important to me.''

"I don't want to take any of that away from you. I just want to be a part of your life. Whatever part you're willing to share.''

She glanced down at her hands, surprised to see them clenched in her lap. She forced herself to unclench them. "We'll see,'' she finally whispered, knowing that she couldn't run from what had happened today. The life she had known with Tony would never be the same, now that he knew the truth.

Cole sat in his study late that evening. He'd stayed there for two reasons. One, to give Allison plenty of time and privacy should she want to use their shared tub. And, two, to be there when Tony returned. As large as the ranch was, there was a possibility that the boy had lost his bearings and headed off in the wrong direction. He'd give him another hour. If he wasn't home by then, he'd go looking for him.

Allison had been upset when Tony hadn't shown up by dinnertime. Cole had reassured her that he couldn't have gotten too lost, since the road they had taken to the creek was one of the main ranch roads and easily followed. Cole figured that Tony would be home when he was ready to face people again.

He'd been waiting almost half an hour when Cole heard the front door ease open and quietly close. He tossed down the pen he'd been making notes with and admitted to himself how relieved he was to know he'd guessed correctly. He walked with a silent tread to the hallway door and looked out. Because of the hall light he had no difficulty seeing Tony as he tiptoed across the tiled floor toward the stairway.

"I thought you might be hungry," Cole said in a low voice that froze Tony in his tracks, "so I had Angie make up a plate of food for you. Why don't we go warm it up?"

Slowly Tony turned to face Cole. His eyes were red and swollen, his face dirty. Exhaustion was etched in every line of his body, but his gaze was steady and clear. Tony had met his ghosts during the past few hours and had faced them.

In that moment, the man he would become was there in the boy's face.

Cole headed toward the kitchen and prayed that Tony would follow. He found the heavily laden plate in the refrigerator and placed it in the microwave. Without looking around he said, "What would you like to drink?" in a casual voice. He hid his relief when he heard Tony answer.

"Milk, if you have it."

After he poured the milk and placed the warmed food in front of Tony, Cole rummaged through the pantry and found the cake he knew was there. He cut two big chunks off and placed them on cake plates. By the time he came out, Tony was busy eating. Cole poured himself a glass of milk and found a fork, then seated himself across the small kitchen table from Tony.

He silently ate his cake and waited. Tony methodically ate every bite of food on his plate, then devoured the cake with no sign of diminished appetite. Cole hid his smile. He remembered the appetite he'd had at that age.

"I guess I owe you an apology for running off like that," Tony finally said in a gruff voice.

"Well, I'll admit your mother was quite worried when you didn't show up for dinner. She said you're not one to miss a meal."

Tony's mouth quirked into a half smile and he finally raised his gaze to meet Cole's. "Yeah. She's right."

"It's not surprising, really. Your body is changing and growing at a rapid rate. You're almost grown."

"I bet it was a shock for you to find out that you had a son, wasn't it?"

So he'd had time to think about other people's feelings as well as his own. A good sign. "Yes, it was."

"I remember how you acted that day at the beach. How did you know?"

Cole smiled, remembering his shocked reaction. "You looked just like Cody did at your age. It was like seeing him all over again."

Tony nodded, looking down at his plate. "My mom used to tell me that I looked like my dad. But I don't think I look much like you."

"Don't you? Well, maybe it's more of a family resemblance."

"Is that why you invited us to come visit, because I'm your son?"

"Partly," Cole admitted. "I wanted to get to know you better, there's no doubt about that. I also wanted to spend some time with your mother."

Tony nodded, his eyes meeting Cole's, then glancing away. "Yeah, I kinda figured that."

"Your mother's had a rough time of it, through no fault of her own."

"I guess so."

"You probably won't be surprised to hear that I love your mother very much. I always have. Losing her was a devastating blow to me. It came at a time when I'd already been knocked to my knees by other equally devastating blows. I suppose that's why I did nothing about looking for her. I thought she had chosen to leave, that she didn't want to be with me anymore, so I made myself accept her absence in my life.'' He took a sip of his milk. ''Now that I know the truth, I want to make up for what she's gone through, if she'll let me. I'd like to make things a little easier for her.''

Tony nodded, as though understanding Cole's need to make amends, then offered his comment. ''My mom's pretty independent, you know.''

Cole recognized the man-to-man tone of voice and respected it. ''Yes, I know.''

''I guess she felt she had to make it on her own.''

''I guess so.''

Tony straightened his shoulders. ''The thing is, I've always felt guilty because she had to work so hard to take care of me.''

''There's no reason for that, you know. Allison loves you very much. She told me today that she didn't know how she would have survived without you all these years. Without you, she would have been totally alone.''

Tony was quiet for several moments, then slowly smiled. ''I've been company for her, huh?''

''You've been family for her. Family is very important to Allison. Just as it is to me.''

Tony studied him for quite a spell before he asked, ''Do you intend to marry her?''

''There's nothing I'd like more.''

''Have you asked her?''

''Yes. But she isn't ready to give me an answer.''

''If you two got married, would we live here on the ranch?''

"We'd probably divide our time between here and Austin, where my headquarters is."

Tony glanced around the kitchen. "This place has been in the family for a long time, hasn't it?"

"Yes, it has."

"I'd like to learn more about it."

"Your Uncle Cameron can tell you just about anything you want to know about the place."

"Do your brothers know about me?"

"Yes."

"And they don't care?"

Cole grinned. "They're delighted."

Tony smiled. "You know something? I think I'm gonna like being a part of a family."

A lump suddenly formed in Cole's throat so that he had to clear it before he answered. "I'm glad, son. Really glad."

Allison stood looking out the bedroom window, watching the activity near the barn. Although the sun had been up less than an hour, Cole and Tony were ready to ride out.

In the two weeks she and Tony had been at the ranch, he and Cole had become inseparable. Tony had unconsciously picked up Cole's mannerisms, his walk, even the way he rode a horse.

The pain in her chest was intense. Her son was rapidly becoming a full-fledged Callaway who no longer needed her. Had he always yearned to have a man in his life? If so, he'd carefully kept it from her, accepting their situation with a minimum of comment.

Cole had kept his agreement. Not once had he come to her room again, nor entered the shared bathroom when she was there. He was friendly enough when she saw him, but that was seldom, since he and Tony spent most of their days away from the Big House. Each evening over dinner Allison listened with a smile as Tony regaled her with tales of his day. Most of his sentences began with "Cole says," or "Cole thinks," or "Cole suggests" and Allison found herself biting her lip to keep from saying something to them.

After all, what could she say? She'd been aware that Cole had wanted to get to know his son and she'd told Cole to leave her alone.

Well, now she knew what her life would be like if she were to accept Cole's proposal of marriage. He would have his son. She would fade into the background of their lives.

Allison turned away from the window. She couldn't do that. Not now. Perhaps if she had married Cole fifteen years ago, as soon as she'd graduated from high school, she would have been willing to stay at home.

Those fifteen years had made her into another woman... an independent woman who was used to looking after herself. She didn't want to lose her identity by becoming one of the Callaway women.

She was Allison Alvarez. She owned a gallery in Mason, Texas. She was ready to return home.

Allison was in the family room when she heard Tony and Cole come into the house from the back. Glancing at her watch, she realized they had decided to come home for lunch. She tossed down the magazine she'd been thumbing through and walked into the hallway.

"Hi," she said, leaning against the open doorway.

"Oh, hi, Mom. You should have come with us. We found some baby armadillos."

Cole paused beside her and said, "I peeked in this morning to see if you might want to go but you were sleeping so peacefully I didn't have the heart to wake you."

When he stood so close to her, she had trouble thinking clearly. Flashes of memory inundated her of Cole in the tub with her, of Cole leaning over her, of Cole—

She straightened, edging away from him and spoke to Tony. "I called Suzanne this morning and told her we'd be home this evening."

"But, Mom—"

"I thought—"

Both Cole and Tony stopped speaking and looked at each other, then at her. Cole said, "I'm sorry. I forgot about your shop. You've been missing it, haven't you?"

"Yes."

"But, Mom, Cole said that—"

"I know what I said, Tony. I guess I lost track of the days. If your mom needs to get back to work, then we'll have to postpone our plans."

She lifted her head and looked at him. "I'm sure you have work that needs attention as well."

Cole nodded. "That's true, although I've been able to handle a great deal over the phone."

Tony dropped his head. "I guess I've been selfish, expecting you to spend all your time with me."

The unhappiness in his voice tore at Allison. It was at that moment that she knew what she had to do. "If Cole agrees, I see no reason why you can't spend the summer with him. Both of you have a great deal of catching up to do."

Both pairs of eyes met hers with equal intensity. Tony's dark ones shone with happiness. "Oh, wow! Could I really?"

"If Cole agrees."

Cole's blue-green gaze glittered. "Is that what you want?" he finally asked.

"It's not a matter of what I want, necessarily. I just know that Tony isn't ready to go home, and I need to get back. I was offering an alternative."

"I'd like to stay if you'll let me," Tony said to his father, his eagerness apparent.

Cole never took his eyes off Allison. "Let me think about it, Tony. I want to discuss it more fully with your mother."

Tony glanced at the two adults who were staring at each other, suddenly becoming aware of the tension between them. "Sure. No problem," he said in an offhand voice, then went up the stairs to his room, leaving them alone.

"What is it?" Cole asked. "What's wrong?" He reached out as though to touch her face, then dropped his hand.

"There's nothing wrong. I can't ask Suzanne to continue to work without relieving her of some of the responsibility."

"Are you sure you want to leave Tony with me?"

She lifted her chin. "He's your son. He's a Callaway. He needs to understand what that means."

"Are you angry with me?"

"Why should I be?"

"Because I've spent so much time with him these past two weeks."

"Wasn't that the purpose of this visit?"

"I wanted to be with you, too, but you've made excuses every time we invited you to come along. Then I finally stopped asking."

"I thought it better for the two of you to talk without my being there."

"Allison—"

His low tone caused a shiver to race up her spine and she knew she was going to have to get away from him before she betrayed herself.

"If it won't be too much trouble, I'd appreciate it if you'd take me back to Mason this afternoon," she said, turning toward the stairs.

"Allison, we need to talk."

She turned back and looked at him. "About what?"

"About us."

"There is no us, Cole. Whatever we had ended fifteen years ago. We're two different people now with our own lives. I'm glad that Tony is going to have the summer with you. I know it's important for you both."

"I was hoping that you and I could—"

She interrupted him before he could finish. "No. I can't go back to being that young girl, Cole. I'm happy with the way my life is now."

"I'm not asking you to give up your work, you know. Since I spend so much time in Austin, we could buy you a gallery there. I thought we might look around for a larger place to live than my condo, one with room for a studio. I want you to be happy, Allison."

"Then take me home."

What could he say to that?

Cole forced himself to nod and turn away while she continued up the stairs. He loved her so much that he ached with it. He walked into his study and sat down, staring at the top of his desk without seeing it. He hadn't allowed himself to consider the possibility that Allison wouldn't be willing to marry him and make a home together.

He closed his eyes and leaned back in his chair. He knew that she was running because she was afraid—afraid of being hurt, afraid of losing her newly found identity, afraid of making a mistake.

Didn't she know that he understood her fears? Didn't she know that he could appreciate her uncertainties for the simple reason that he shared them?

He knew that he had to let her go, but it was the hardest task he'd ever had to face.

Eleven

The deer hunters were everywhere she looked in Mason that particular November morning when Allison opened the gallery for the day. Business had been brisk this season. Several of the hunters had stopped in and purchased either photographs of the area or some of her smaller sculptures these past few weeks. She had kept busy filling commissioned orders. However, she intended to take the weekend off to rest.

The high school football team had a game in Mason that night. Tony would be playing, at least for part of the game.

She smiled when she thought of her son. He was growing up so fast. Cole had called her in July and suggested that she meet them in San Antonio to celebrate Tony's birthday. Coward that she was, she couldn't face Cole again so soon.

She'd talked to Tony and explained that she couldn't get away, but that she would plan a special outing in the fall when he returned. He had accepted her explanations without comment. She had no idea how Cole had reacted.

She knew that she would have to get used to seeing him now that they were going to share Tony. The problem was that she wasn't certain how she would manage. Just the sound of his voice on the phone set her pulse pounding and caused a distinct shortness of breath in her lungs. Cole called the house with alarming regularity to talk to Tony. She'd gotten to the point that she wouldn't answer the phone. Since most of the calls were for Tony, anyway, he'd never commented on her behavior.

She didn't want to react to Cole that way! He was part of her past, that's all. She'd made her decision last summer and it had been the right one for her. It was just taking her emotions a little longer to accept her choice.

During the call he'd made in July he point-blank asked if she was pregnant and had not disguised his disappointment when she'd told him that she wasn't.

Thank God she wasn't pregnant.

She couldn't have handled the idea of marrying Cole because she was pregnant, not after spending fifteen years of her life thinking he hadn't wanted her when she was pregnant the first time.

Everything had worked out for all of them. She had her life, her work, her gallery. Tony had come back to Mason in September and announced to his friends that he had spent the summer with Cole Callaway and that they were friends. She wondered how the townspeople would react if they knew the truth?

She stepped inside the shop. There was a real nip in the air this morning and she was glad to get inside. As soon as she warmed up her office, she began working on a new sculpture—a wild horse standing on a bluff looking off into the distance. The only peace Allison found anymore was when she was working with her clay. She spent her day working quietly in the backroom while Suzanne handled any customers who came in. By the time she got home that evening, she was feeling more relaxed than she had in weeks. Her sculpture was coming along very well. She had scarcely thought of Cole all day.

Tony had already eaten by the time she got home, since he wasn't supposed to eat too close to game time. He was excited about the upcoming game. Tonight they were playing their archrivals from a neighboring town.

"I've gotta go, Mom," Tony said, giving her a quick kiss on the cheek. "See ya at the game."

She smiled. "You're not supposed to be looking into the stands, you know. You're supposed to be paying attention to what's going on with the ball."

"Hey, no problem. I can do both," he said with a grin. He took off, slamming the front door. She shook her head, wondering if he would ever slow down.

She heated the remains of dinner from the night before, ate them, then headed toward the bedroom to change into warmer clothes. By the time she had her turtleneck sweater, vest, wool skirt and knee boots on, she figured she'd be warm enough when she added her coat. Trying to decide what to do with her hair, she had finally parted it in preparation for a braid when she heard the front doorbell.

She hadn't a clue who would be visiting at this hour. Everyone in Mason knew about the game. All other activities were put on hold during football season. She let go of her hair, allowing it to drape around her shoulders like a shawl and went to the door.

When she opened the door, she froze.

"Hello, Allison. May I come in?"

It was Cole. Stunned, she stepped back so that he could enter. She watched as he walked down the hall and into the family room, then hastily closed the door and followed him. When she entered the room he turned away from the sliding glass door and said, "You're looking good. How've you been?"

"All right." She couldn't say the same about him. He looked as though he'd lost twenty pounds. His face was drawn and there were definite traces of gray over his ears.

"I know you're wondering what I'm doing here after you asked me not to come," he began, only to be distracted. He walked over and picked up Tony's latest school picture, which she'd framed and set on a bookshelf. "When was this taken?"

"About three weeks ago. He just brought that one home Monday. He saved you one."

He smiled. "Good. I'd love to have it."

His smile almost undid her, it seemed so familiar. He was so much a part of her. How could she expect herself to push him out of her mind?

"I'll be right back," she said, grateful for a few moments by herself. When she returned with the picture set aside for him, Cole took it carefully in his hands, as though she'd given him a priceless object that needed fragile handling. He stared at Tony's likeness for several minutes before he finally said, "Thank you," without looking up.

"Why did you come, Cole?" she asked.

When he raised his head, his eyes glittered with moisture. "I need to talk to you about something and I thought it would be better to discuss it in person. But I guess the real truth is, I couldn't stay away any longer."

He turned his back to her and walked over to the sliding door once more. "I had to see you, to see if this is really what you want for us. I can't imagine not being in your life somewhere. I've picked up the phone a hundred times to let you know I was thinking of you, and realized that if I called you whenever I thought of you, I'd be on the phone all the time."

"Don't, Cole," she pleaded softly.

"Don't what?" he asked, turning to look at her. "Don't think? Don't feel? Don't ache to hold you again? Do you have any idea how many nights I lay awake wishing you were there to touch, to hold, to talk to, to love?" He looked away again. "I even subscribed to your local newspaper, so I could see your weekly ad, read every item of news just in case you or Tony are mentioned. When I read that there was a game tonight I decided to accept Tony's invitation to see him play. I've been turning him down, thinking it would be too painful to see you. I decided that nothing is as painful as not seeing you at all. So I'm here."

She bit her bottom lip in an effort not to respond. He was hurting. She could see it in his face, hear it in his voice.

"I thought that having Tony in your life would be enough," she said, finally.

"Enough?"

She turned away. "He's your son and—"

"And you're my love, and I want you both, can't you understand that? What is it you think I'm going to do that you can't accept?"

She sighed. "I'm not sure. I've thought about it over the past few months and I guess what I'm afraid of is losing my identity."

"I can't take that away from you, you know."

"Perhaps not," she admitted.

He nodded, seemingly content that she was at least looking at their situation.

"One of the reasons I wanted to see you in person was to let you know that I want both of you to come to the ranch for Christmas. Cameron is doing better now. He's working again, dividing his time between his office and the ranch. Letty's home and, Allison, she's different. She really is. She had no idea about your pregnancy. She knows what she did was wrong. I think you'll see the changes."

"I don't know, Cole. I'll have to think about it."

"That's something I guess. In the meantime, I'd like to go to the game with you tonight. I want to sit there with you and the rest of the parents and cheer our son on."

She almost smiled at the determination in his voice. "All right."

"You aren't going to argue?"

She shrugged. "Cole, I learned a long time ago not to argue with you when your mind's made up."

"Well, that's a relief," he replied with a grin.

"I need to finish braiding my hair. Then we need to go if we're going to be there for the kickoff."

He helped her with her coat when she returned, and tugged her beret so that it sat saucily over one eye. "You look about sixteen, yourself."

"Thank God I'm not," she said, allowing him to take her hand and lead her out to his car.

"The idea of going back and doing it again doesn't appeal to you?" he asked, tucking her into the car before walking around to the driver's side.

"Living through all of that once was more than enough."

"But maybe we could change things the second time around."

"I doubt it. Given the same set of circumstances, I don't see things changing all that much. Human nature being what it is, we would probably all act out our roles in a similar way."

"A rather dismal thought. Surely we've learned something from the first time."

"Ah, but we wouldn't be given the advantage of remembering. It would all be new to us."

He reached over and took her hand, placing it on his thigh and dropping his hand over it. They rode down the hill toward the football field in that position.

"There is something else I need to discuss with you while I'm here."

"All right."

"I've been approached to run for governor in the upcoming election."

"You'd make a good governor."

"Actually, I'm seriously thinking of disqualifying myself."

She looked around at him in surprise. "Why?"

"Because of Tony."

"I don't understand."

"A politician's past is open to scrutiny once he announces his candidacy. The other side would like nothing better than to get hold of a juicy piece of news such as Tony's birth."

"But, Cole, they couldn't prove a thing. There's no way to tie you with Tony, or to me, for that matter."

"You're missing my point, honey. I want to tie myself to both of you. I don't intend to deny that he's my son. I'm damned proud of it."

"That's political suicide. You just said—"

"I know what I just said. That's why I want to talk to you about it. I don't want you and Tony hurt by something that might come out of the campaign. So I wanted to talk to you and get your views about it. I'm not that fired up about running for a public office, anyway. I can do just as much in other ways. The guy sittin' out there on top is the one who gets all the potshots aimed at him. I just needed to talk to you about it. Your opinion is important to me."

"Oh, Cole. I don't know what to say. You'll have to decide what to do."

"Would it make a difference to you, Allison? Being with you is more important to me than anything. I've been trying to give you space over the past few months, but I'm not sure I can keep this up much longer."

She looked away from him. So he hadn't accepted her decision as final. Was she relieved to know that, to know that he still wanted her as much as ever? Why was she so afraid to accept what he was offering to her?

"I don't know," she whispered out loud.

"You don't know what? Whether you love me? Whether you're willing to marry me? What?"

"I'm afraid," she finally admitted.

"So am I. But more than anything else, I'm afraid of having to spend the rest of my life without you."

"Here's the parking area," she pointed out, grateful that there was a timely interruption to the conversation.

By the time they found some seats the team had run out on the field and was warming up. The night was cool but pleasant. Everyone was excited about the upcoming contest, and the stadium was noisy.

Cole seemed to fit right in with the others. She introduced him to more than a dozen people between the time they bought their tickets and the time they found their seats. Some people recognized him and spoke. He looked relaxed and friendly. If he hadn't been gripping her hand like a drowning man she would have had no idea he was nervous.

"If you don't ease up on my hand, gangrene is going to set in," she whispered. "Circulation was cut off some time ago."

"There he is!" he said suddenly. "Over there." He pointed with his other hand without releasing his death grip. She started prying his fingers from her hand and he looked down in surprise. "Oh! I'm sorry. Was I hurting you?"

She flexed her cramped fingers and smiled. "Tools of the trade, you know. I've gotta be careful." Cole took her hand, and ignoring the fact that they were the object of many an interested observer, brought her fingers to his lips and kissed them, one by one.

"Is that better?"

"Cole!" she whispered through a smile. "You're embarrassing me." She tugged on her hand, but he held on to it, tucking it firmly between his elbow and his side. She turned away in time to see Tony, while doing warm-ups, look toward the stands. She waved with her other hand and he saw her. His smile lit up his face and then froze with astonishment when he saw Cole. After a pause, he clasped his hands and raised them above his head.

Cole laughed.

"What's that all about?"

"I think he's glad I came to see him. I'm glad, too, but I have to admit I've been a little nervous about seeing you again."

"Does Tony know that?"

"I may have mentioned it to him a time or two," he said in a casual voice.

"Something tells me I've been set up here," she murmured, watching her son speculatively. Once again he glanced up in the stands, this time giving her a thumbs-up signal. She glanced around and discovered that Cole was wearing an identical grin to his son's. She shook her head and said, "You two are just alike."

"Really?" Cole asked, obviously pleased.

"I wouldn't be so proud, if I were you."

"You really think he's like me?"

"Who are we kidding here? Of course he's like you. The older he gets the more he looks like you. He has to know the truth every time he looks into a mirror."

Allison had never seen Cole with quite that expression on his face before. He glowed with pride. She knew then that she had never loved this man who clutched her hand to his side as much as she did right at that moment. For a brief minute the knowledge was almost overwhelming. Now that he was here, she didn't see how she could let him walk away again. Ready or not, she was going to have to accept that this man would always be a part of her. No one had been fooled by her denials, least of all her heart.

The game was in the third quarter and Mason was a touchdown behind when a whistle ended a play where several players were in a pile. Cole came to his feet. "Tony was the one with the ball. Is he all right?" he muttered.

This was the part that Allison hated. She tried not to worry about injuries, but the game was rough enough without the extra adrenaline flowing tonight, as they fought against their archrivals. Most of the people in the stands were on their feet.

When the field cleared one player still lay on the field. It was Tony. Allison gave a gasp and frantically started to climb over people, absently excusing herself. Cole was right behind her. They were on the sidelines by the time he was carried off on a stretcher. The volunteer ambulance squad took him to the ambulance where they began to check him over.

"Is he all right?" she asked, following them.

"He's unconscious, Allison," one of the men said. "I think we'd better take him into Fredericksburg to the hospital, to be safe."

That was over forty miles away. Cole took over. "You ride with them in the ambulance, honey. I'll be right behind you in the car."

Never had Allison felt so frightened. As an energetic little boy, Tony had gotten several scrapes and bumps in his life, but nothing like this. She wanted him safe. She wanted him to open his eyes and give her that special grin of his, reassuring her that he was all right.

Never had she felt more alone.

Riding in the back of the ambulance through the night, she reminded herself that for the first time in a very long while she was not alone... Cole was there.

She didn't have to go through this alone. Not now. Not ever. She took a deep breath and let go... let go of her fears, her indecisions, her apprehension about the future.

She didn't have to do anything alone, not anymore.

By the time the ambulance reached the hospital, Tony had regained consciousness, but he remained groggy. They took him into emergency for tests and X rays.

Allison was giving the admissions clerk information on him when Cole walked in. In the most natural gesture of her life, Allison held out her hand to him. "He's with the doctor now but they don't think it's too serious. Perhaps a minor concussion. He was awake in the ambulance and didn't have any problem answering their questions.''

Cole closed his eyes for a moment. She could feel the surge of relief that flowed through him. ''Thank God.''

Yes. Thank God. For so many things, she realized.

''Will he have to stay overnight?'' he asked, looking around.

''We don't know yet.''

By the time the doctor got through with him, Tony had been pronounced well enough to go home that night, provided he took it easy over the weekend. Allison didn't think she was going to have any trouble keeping him down.

When she and Tony came out of the examining room Cole was waiting. With no hesitation Tony walked into Cole's arms and clung. Allison saw Cole's eyes fill with tears before he dropped his head and hugged his son.

When Tony finally raised his head, his grin was crooked. ''When I invited you to come see me play, I didn't mean to knock myself out showing off.''

Cole laughed and Allison could feel herself relaxing.

''I bet you have the granddaddy of all headaches about now,'' Cole responded.

''Just about.''

''I'll take you home,'' Cole said, still with his arm around him. He glanced at Allison. ''Ready?''

She looked at the two of them, standing there together. What had she been so afraid of?

''Yes . . . I believe I am.''

By the time they reached Mason, Tony was asleep in the back seat. He offered little resistance when Cole helped him out of the car. Following the two of them up to the front door, Allison suddenly realized that Tony was almost as tall as Cole. Somehow the thought that her son was no longer a child swept through her and she almost wept. Where had all the years gone?

"Do you need any help getting ready for bed, Tony?" she asked once they were inside.

"Uh-uh. I'll see you later," he mumbled, and started down the hall. He paused halfway and looked back. "Thanks for coming to see me, Cole," he said. "Even though I didn't finish the game," he added wryly.

"I'm glad I was there. I'm just sorry you were hurt."

Tony shrugged. "It comes with the territory, you know?"

Cole nodded. "Yep. I know."

"Night, Mom," he mumbled, then went on into his room.

Cole and Allison were left by the front door. "Would you like some coffee before you head back?"

He stretched and yawned. "You mean you're going to insist on my leaving tonight?"

She thought about that for a moment. She did have some things she needed to say before he left. "I suppose you could sleep in the guest room, if you'd like."

He grinned. "I'd like."

She turned away to make them some coffee. Cole's grins were next to impossible to resist, and she needed to keep her wits about her. While she measured the coffee and water, she said, "I can't tell you how much it meant to me tonight, having you there." She turned and came toward him. "I can't remember ever having been so afraid for someone in quite that way. I felt so help-less . . . and alone."

"I know what you mean."

They stood there looking at each other for a moment before Allison stepped forward, walking into his arms as though there was no place she would rather be.

Cole could feel his heart thundering in his chest. The sweet scent of her wrapped around him, soothing him. He hugged her to him.

"I love you, sweetheart," he whispered. "So much that I sometimes wonder if I can live with the ache it causes."

She sighed, her contentment obvious as she laid her head on his shoulder. "I'm tired of fighting this thing, Cole. I love you. How could I not love you? I'm raising another Callaway just like you. It continues to amaze me how much he reminds me of you."

He only intended to comfort her with a light kiss, but the moment his lips touched hers, he felt as though he'd gone up in flames. He drew her ever closer to him, loving the feel of her body pressed so intimately against him, wanting her so desperately that he wasn't at all certain he could survive without her.

When he finally lifted his head and looked down at her, her face glowed with a loving radiance that humbled him.

"Does this mean that you'll marry me?" he finally whispered.

She nodded her head, unable to speak.

His next kiss was even more eloquent. He wasn't sure he could let go of her, now that he knew she had agreed to marry him. When he finally paused for air, he decided to risk the next question.

"Would you consider having more children?"

Her eyes opened in a lazy and extremely seductive way. "As a matter of fact, I'd insist on it. I never wanted to raise an only child, but it couldn't be helped. We'd need to have at least a couple more, don't you think?"

With a muffled shout of joy, he picked her up in his arms and carried her over to the sofa. "Oh, I think we can manage." He sat with her on his lap. "When?"

"Well, it takes at least nine months, as you know, and—"

"Not that! I'm asking about marriage. How soon?"

She shook her head. "I have no idea."

"I have several. How about Christmas?"

"So soon?"

"Soon! That's over six weeks away!"

"But there's so much I need to do."

"Why don't we have a quiet family wedding at the ranch? I don't think Cam's going to be in the mood for many festivities this year."

She leaned her forehead against his. "You're right, of course. Maybe we should wait a few months."

"Honey, I've waited fifteen years. Cam will understand." He slid his hand across her breasts, feeling her suddenly catch her breath.

"We can't, Cole. Not tonight. Not here."

He sighed. "You're right. I know you are. It's just that I need you so much."

She smiled. "Just look at what we have to look forward to, though."

"If I can survive the cold showers," he growled and kissed her again, determined to leave no doubt in her mind regarding his desire for her.

Epilogue

The Big House glowed inside and out with Christmas decorations. Inside, the fireplaces burned mesquite wood, scenting the air. Trisha's giggles and delighted squeals echoed along with the Christmas carols playing on the stereo system and the conversations from the many adults standing around in the foyer greeting the new arrivals.

Allison and Tony had just arrived. Cole had gone to get them and was just now setting the last of their luggage inside the door.

The first person's eyes Allison caught were Letitia Callaway's. The woman had aged considerably. Her hair was completely gray. She looked old and tired. Her gaze was almost shy as she looked at Allison.

Allison walked over to the older woman, bringing Tony with her. "Letty, I want you to meet Tony."

The older woman flinched at the familiar name, but she didn't look away. "My, you are a big one, aren't you?" she said, her voice shaking slightly. "You look just like the pictures of your dad at that age. Except for your eyes, of course." She faltered a little on the last words. "You got those beautiful eyes from your grandfather."

Cameron and Cody were both there, Cameron holding Trisha, Cody teasing Rosie who was passing a tray around. But everyone stopped talking and looked at the tableau before them.

Tony took the offered hand and shook it. "I never knew my grandfather," he said in his baritone voice that on occasion slid up an octave.

She nodded slowly. "He was a fine man. A man to be proud of. Wear his name well."

Tony grinned. "I'll try."

Cole walked in at the beginning of their remarks and he held his breath, having no idea what either the crotchety old woman or the outspoken teenager might say to each other.

He breathed a sigh of relief when general greetings were started up once again. "I'll take the luggage up-stairs," Cole said to no one in particular.

He placed Tony's in the room he'd had on their previous visit. He placed Allison's belongings in his room. They would discuss the proprieties later. They would be married in less than a week, and he didn't intend to wait another night for her.

Dinner went well. Everyone was excited to see each other. Cody had been gone for almost two months without telling anyone where or why he'd disappeared. He smiled his familiar cocky smile when asked and had a smart-aleck come-back that told them absolutely nothing.

Although Cameron now spent several days a week in San Antonio, he continued to have Trisha stay at the ranch. She was settled there and comfortable. Everyone doted on her. Cole knew that the child received a great deal of love and attention, but he worried about Cam. He couldn't help it, even though he knew he had to accept Cam's way of dealing with his grief.

"What did you tell them today, Cole?" Cameron asked over dessert and coffee.

"To find somebody else. I had other plans." He took a sip of coffee.

"Good for you," Cameron said with a toasting gesture of his cup. "I'm glad you didn't let them push you around."

"They tried."

"I'm sure they did."

"What are you talking about?" Letty demanded to know.

Cameron explained. "Oh, just some of the guys pushing Cole to run for governor."

Cole's glance met Allison's and he smiled.

Tony's eyes got round. "So you're going to run for governor?"

"No. I don't intend to run."

"Why not?" Tony asked, shocked.

Once again Cole's eyes met Allison's. "I've got more important things to do with my time."

Cody jumped in with a hilarious anecdote that soon had them all laughing.

The subject was not brought up again. Instead the family spent the evening in front of the fireplace, chatting and getting better acquainted with Tony.

When Allison finally decided to go upstairs for the night, she opened the door to her room and was surprised not to see any of her things laid out, or at least her luggage waiting to be unpacked. Puzzled, she walked into the bathroom where she found her toiletries neatly set out. Curious, she peeked into Cole's bedroom.

Her gown was draped at the foot of the bed, with her robe and slippers nearby. She could feel her face grow hot. What did he think he was doing? He wasn't even making a pretense of anything. He was—

The door from the hallway opened and Cole walked in. He glanced around and saw her and a very wicked grin appeared on his face.

"Now, Cole..."

He stalked over to her and grabbed her up in his arms. "Now, Allison," he mimicked.

"You know I can't stay in here with you. What will—"

"Don't give me any of this 'what will people think' routine. In the first place, it's none of their business. In the second place, there's no reason for anyone to know. I put your things away so no one else knows you're here, but even if they did, so what? We'll be married in a few days, so what difference does it make?"

"It isn't that, I just feel that Tony's not going to understand and—"

"On the contrary, Tony is quite understanding. Tony and I had a nice man-to-man talk last night after you went to bed."

"Oh?"

"Yes. I explained how long I'd waited for you and how eager I was for the three of us to become a family. He didn't have a problem with any of it, except to ask why it had taken me so long to convince you!"

"Oh, Cole," she said, recognizing his teasing. "I love you so much."

"Glad to hear it," he growled, hauling her up tight against his body. "What's the possibility of getting you to mention that little tidbit of information more often?"

She touched her lips to his jawline and whispered, "I'm just afraid, that's all."

"Afraid? Of what, for God's sake?"

"All of this is so new to me. I know all about being independent. Now I need to learn how to be a wife."

He brushed his fingertips across her cheek. "You don't have to worry about any of that, you know. I love you, no matter what you do or how you behave."

He reached around to the back of her dress and tugged at the zipper. "I don't want to wait another night for you, love. I've been extraordinarily patient these past few weeks. There's no way I could sleep knowing that you're in the next room."

She began to unbutton his shirt with trembling fingers. She knew exactly what he meant. She'd had a difficult time falling asleep the night before, knowing he was there in her home. Tonight, they didn't have to pretend.

Allison tilted her head back so that she could see his eyes. "Whatever you say, dear," she replied demurely. His shirt fell to the floor and she brushed her palms across his broad chest.

He began to laugh. "I've never heard you so meek. I think I'm going to like your new attitude."

"Enjoy it while you can," she said with a smile, leading him to the bed. "I have some very definite ideas about what I want to do with you."

"Honey, I'm all yours. I always have been."

She gave him a gentle push so that he sat on the bed, then stretched out across it. She reached for his belt buckle. "Cole?"

"Hmm?"

"Do you have an idea when you want to start expanding our family?"

His heated gaze met hers. "The sooner, the better, as far as I'm concerned."

"How about the number?"

"I'd have a dozen more, if that's what you want, honey."

She smiled, her black eyes dancing. "Even for a Texan, that's really bragging."

He grabbed her arm and pulled her down beside him. He turned, holding her to him with his arm and leg over her. "I want whatever you want, darlin', for now and ever more."

She kissed him—a short, hard kiss. Then a second time she softened the kiss to include all the love and tenderness she felt for this man.

"Then I may have to keep you in bed for a while over the next few weeks," she said when she raised her head.

His eyes were as bright as the Christmas lights that surrounded the house.

"Whatever you say, dear," he mimicked, his pleased expression effectively wiping out all the years they had spent apart. The present was much more important.

* * * * *

NORA ROBERTS

Love has a language all its own, and for centuries flowers have symbolized love's finest expression. Discover the language of flowers—and love—in this romantic collection of 48 favorite books by bestselling author Nora Roberts.

Two titles are available each month at your favorite retail outlet.

In September, look for:

All the Possibilities, **Volume #15**
The Heart's Victory, **Volume #16**

In October, look for:

One Man's Art, **Volume #17**
Rules of the Game, **Volume #18**

THE LANGUAGE of LOVE

Collect all 48 titles
and become fluent in

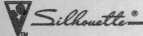
Silhouette ®

™

Take 4 bestselling love stories FREE

Plus get a FREE surprise gift!

SILHOUETTE® Desire™

presents

SONS OF TEXAS
by Annette Broadrick

As rugged as their native land, the Callaway brothers—Cole, Cameron and Cody—are three sinfully sexy heroes ready to ride into your heart.

In September—
LOVE TEXAS STYLE! (SD#734)

In October—
COURTSHIP TEXAS STYLE! (SD#739)

In November—
MARRIAGE TEXAS STYLE! (SD#745)

Don't let these Sons of Texas get away—men as hot as the Texas sun they toil . . . and *romance* . . . under! Only from Silhouette Desire . . .